Contents

MY TUDOR QUEEN

London, England
1501

4th November 1501

I hardly like to make a mark on the beautiful, blank pages of this book, but I must. Mama gave it to me as a parting present so that I could write about this journey from Spain to England. "Don't waste it," she said. "Just write the important things. The big ones."

That was three months ago. It was August when we sailed from Corunna – but how could I write in that terrible storm? We had hardly been at sea for two days when it struck us. People were weeping and praying and being thrown about like dried peas in a baby's rattle. One of our ships sank. I came up to get some air because the smell below decks was so awful, and I saw her roll over helpless as a dead thing, and then the towering waves swallowed her. We were driven back to the Basque coast, with broken masts and rigging washed overboard, and it was a month before the repairs were done and we could start out again. Even then, we were tempest-tossed, but at last we landed in Plymouth.

People came aboard to meet us, and Catherine received them with truly royal dignity. Although she is my childhood friend, I have always known she was a princess – but until that day, I hadn't realized how perfectly she can play the part. The English were delighted with her, and seemed impressed that she asked to go to a church to give thanks for our safe arrival, even before we could change our clothes or have something to eat. She is not yet sixteen but she has great self-possession.

Would Mama think these were big things? I'm sure she would be impressed by the great procession in which we have slowly made our way from the West Country to London. Horses and carriages, litters and baggage-waggons and attendants, soldiers, courtiers, ladies, pages, jesters – and Catherine herself, Catherine of Aragon, on her way to wed Prince Arthur, eldest son of the King of England.

But there have been little things as well, yellow leaves on the trees that stand everywhere, and skies full of birdsong. Grass and tall weeds, rain and mud. Oh, the mud! Mama warned me that England was a wet place, but I never imagined such mud. Perhaps it will be better in London, but so far the journey has been heavy going. The horses have floundered knee-deep sometimes, struggling to get a foothold, and the carriages lurch and splash, and sometimes we have had to stop because of a broken axle or lost wheel. We've all been grateful for an occasional dry day of autumn sunshine.

I have been wretchedly homesick sometimes, longing for warmth and the smell of Spanish cooking. And Mama. When will I see her again? But at least Uncle Rodrigo is in London. When I was small, I used to call him Uncle Rod, but Mama warned me not to use that pet name in front of the courtiers. To them he is Doctor Rodrigo Gonsalez De Puebla, ambassador to England from Catherine's parents, King Ferdinand and Queen Isabella of Spain. He has a son whom I have never met, called Gonsalvo, so at least I will have some sort of family in this strange land.

Tonight we are lodged at the manor house of some lord, not far from London. It is cold in this room although a smoky fire burns in the hearth. The candle flame gutters in the wind that blows in through the glassless windows. Our windows in Spain are not glazed, either, but it is different for us. Wrought-iron grilles keep thieves out and let in whatever air there is to cool our sun-hot walls and floors. These English are a mystery to me. How do they endure the cold? It is dirty, too. The floors are strewn with rushes, fresh ones being scattered over the filth and dropped food of the previous day, and although the dishes are of gold or silver plate, the noblemen do not always bother to go outside or to the retiring room when they need to relieve themselves. They behave, it seems to me, very much as the dogs do which skulk round the tables and snatch at thrown scraps of meat.

Perhaps it is as well that I write my diary in Spanish! It has a hasp and lock on its leather cover, too, so it is safe, I hope, from prying eyes. I could equally well write in English if I chose. That is why I am here, for my skill as an interpreter. The Queen would not have sent me simply as Catherine's childhood friend, or because we share a love of embroidery. Mama is the chief embroideress at the Spanish court, and is necessarily quite close to the Queen, but Isabella has no use for sentiment, except when it comes to the passion she feels for her religion. "Isabella the Catholic", they call her, perhaps in fear as much as in admiration. When Catherine and I were small, she rode against the Moors in full armour at the head of her troops, and she will tolerate no wavering from what she considers the true Church.

These things are not for me to comment on. My place here has nothing to do with embroidery or friendship, though both of these will be useful. I serve as Catherine's interpreter, and stand close by her when the important and gorgeously dressed nobles present themselves, murmuring the meaning of what they say so that only she can hear. That way, at least she can smile or look grave as is suitable, and trot out her few English phrases in the right place. "Yes . . . no . . . thank you." Poor Catherine.

What am I saying? How absurd to call her poor when she is a princess of Castile, her mother's youngest and favourite daughter! Yet I do pity her, somehow. She seems so young, though she is only six months behind me, her birthday on December 16th, mine on the tenth day of June. We look very different, though. She is all honey and cream, with skin the colour of a just-ripening peach, while I am as dark as an olive. Papa was a scholar and teacher, and I take after him in many ways. I still miss him, though it is three years since he died. I inherited his bookishness and love of learning – though nothing else, for he was never a rich man – and I think the Queen considered me a good influence on her frivolous-minded daughter.

Catherine always wanted to be active, and lessons bored her. She would sit pouting over her Latin grammar (though goodness knows Latin is easy enough, being so close to Spanish), twisting a strand of her honey-gold hair round her finger, and if voices sounded from the courtyard below she would jump up at once to see who it was, and then laugh and wave from the window. She should have been a boy, I think. She was much happier with the practical subjects which her mother insisted on, riding and shooting, falconry and archery. She even quite liked the domestic skills of baking and weaving and spinning. And she loves embroidery. My mother taught us our needlework. We used to sit outside sometimes, in the shade of the feathery pepper trees, stitching our designs of leaves and tendrils and curving arabesques while we chattered of whatever we fancied.

Mostly, we used only one colour – black or dark red – which stood out on the white cloth, but from what I have seen here, the English delight in a riot of scarlets and purples, blues and gold. I think they see things differently. In the burning sun of Spain, one sees through eyes half-shut against the glare. Things are silhouetted: the curls of wrought iron, the intricate droop of the acacia tree. One never need narrow the eyes here. The light is gentle, the colours a constant shifting of greens, blues and greys highlighted by bright berries and sky-reflecting water.

These are little things – Mama would scold me. The candle is almost burned down, I must go to bed.

5th November 1501

We have come to a place called Dogmersfield, and hardly had we entered the house when in rushed a Spanish ambassador – not my uncle, but a man called Don Pedro de Ayala – to warn us that the King himself was outside, demanding to meet with Catherine.

Doña Elvira was horrified. She is Catherine's duenna (a sort of governess), ferocious at the best of times – and this was not the best. Poor thing, she is bruised black and blue from being jolted about in a carriage. I'm so glad I'm young enough to ride! Anyway, Doña Elvira heaved herself to her feet and went out grumbling, and we heard her protests being translated for the King. "No, Your Majesty, it is not possible to see the princess. It is not the custom for a bride to be seen by the groom or his father before the wedding day." It was a polite translation – her Spanish was a lot more forthright. Don Pedro explained that the princess was resting, but the King cut in, "I don't care if she's in her bed asleep. I am coming in to see her."

Doña Elvira came back with her face as red as a peony – she is not used to being argued with. And behind her came King Henry himself – King Henry VII of England – a lean, determined man with a mouth set like a trap.

Catherine was not in the least flustered. She swept him a low curtsey, and his rat-trap mouth relaxed into a smile as he kissed her hand then stood back to look at her. Carefully, he noted her trim figure and the dancer's grace with which she stands and moves, her small hands and feet, her creamy skin and clear grey eyes. His own eyes ran down the long flow of her honey-coloured hair and his smile broadened. He looked, I thought, like a horse trader, well-pleased by the thoroughbred filly he has bought.

He and Catherine conversed (if one can call it that) in Latin, neither of them knowing a word of the other's language, and Doña Elvira stood with folded arms and a thunderous face. Half an hour later, Prince Arthur himself arrived with a large entourage, and he, too, came in to inspect his bride.

Catherine looked at him, then carefully avoided meeting my gaze. I knew why. Arthur, at fourteen, is a slender boy, little more than a child. He has great charm and sweetness, but his shoulders are narrow and any emotion brings a blush to his pale cheeks. He is as tall as Catherine, but looks much less strong. Everyone was scrupulously courteous, and if Catherine is disappointed, she will never, ever say so.

7th November 1501

Tonight we are in the city of London, lodged at the Bishop's Palace. There is glass in the windows here, for which I am grateful.

We were escorted into the city by a great cohort of the Duke of Buckingham's men. They were dressed in scarlet and black so that they looked like glowing coals, and the long red banners above them flickered like flames. And at St George's Fields we all came to a halt, for another troop of men was approaching. And at their head rode young Henry Tudor, brother of Prince Arthur, sent by his father to greet us.

What a boy! Only ten years old, but already as tall as his older brother, and far stronger and more confident. He swung himself from his horse, tossed the reins to a servant whom he did not even look at, then advanced towards us with a smile on his handsome face, doffed his feathered cap and bowed low. One of our ladies murmured quietly in Spanish, "A pity this boy is not the elder." Several of the others nodded and Catherine, curtseying to young Harry, as they call him, looked up to meet his gaze and could not look away.

Shivers ran down my back. In that moment, the pair of them seemed to belong together, young though Prince Harry is – but of course, the children of royalty are not free to follow the wishes of their hearts. In just a week from now, Catherine will marry the older brother, Arthur, and nothing will alter that.

Evidently the people of London are all set for a great fiesta. Flags and banners fly everywhere, and fantastic arches have been built across the streets, painted to look like bridges or castles, and wherever I look there are elaborate designs that link the arms of England with the crimson pomegranate of Granada. It's all very exciting – and I'm so proud of Uncle Rod. I know from his letters to Mama, who is his niece, how hard he has worked for many years to bring about this marriage between England and Spain. I look forward so much to seeing him.

9th November 1501

At last! Uncle Rod came to the Bishop's Palace today. He is much older than I remember him, and somehow not as big. I used to think he was a tall man, but I suppose that was because I was only small. He is barely my height now, and rather dumpy in shape, with his coat buttons not quite meeting across his tummy. Properly speaking, he is my *great* uncle, of course, but I had never thought of that before. His son, Gonsalvo, came as well, a dark-haired man much older than me, together with his wife, Bianca, and their baby son, Miguel. Gonsalvo is a lawyer, like Uncle Rod, but he shook his head when I asked if he was at court, and said he would rather deal with the rogues of the street than such a parcel of monkeys. Uncle Rod frowned at him and told me to take no notice.

Both of them are much annoyed that Don Pedro de Ayala has come to London. His job was supposed to be in Scotland, arranging a marriage between the Scottish king, James IV, and another of King Henry's children, Princess Margaret. Gonsalvo says Don Pedro probably finds it more comfortable here than in the rough, cold court of Scotland. Can it really be colder than it is here? I tremble to think of it.

12th November 1501

People stare at us wherever we go. I suppose it is because we look different from the tall, pale English. I heard a man murmur to his companion that we looked like "pigmei Ethiopes". He spoke in Latin, but did he imagine we were too uncivilized to understand? "Pygmy Ethiopians" indeed! How rude! I asked who the man was, and learned that his name is Thomas More. It makes me wonder what the King, for all his courtesies, really thinks of us.

We met Prince Arthur's sisters this afternoon, and I liked them both. Margaret, who is to marry James of Scotland, is twelve. She's a merry girl, more like her brother Harry than the slender Arthur, but little

Mary is quite different. She's only six, a very pretty child with curling fair hair, but very serious. "I will sing for you," she said. And she did, amazingly well, her little voice true and sweet. They say she will marry the Duke of Milan's son when she is old enough – unless, of course, they've found someone more important by that time.

I'm glad I was not born a royal child. It must be hard to grow up knowing you will be given to a husband you have never met and may not even like – and at such an early age, too. I heard yesterday that King Henry's mother was only twelve years old when he was born, and she was so injured in having him that she was never able to bear another child. The woman who told me shook her head, not so much in pity as in disapproval. "Spoiled," she said, as if a queen is only valued for the children she produces. How odd that they are laden with jewels and fine clothes and yet their function is no different from that of the cow in the farmyard!

If Catherine is aware of these things, she never mentions them. We talk about the coming wedding, of course, but only in terms of dresses and flowers and whether she will really wear her hair loose as the English insist. She is the centre of all attention and loves every moment of it, but people only flock round her because she is the Princess of Aragon. They do not know Catherine as a real person and I suspect that they don't want to. It's not their concern.

This afternoon there was a great argument about hoops. The Spanish style is to wear a hoop under one's skirt so it stands out from the body, but the English don't do this. They let the dress fall about one's natural form, and we are enchanted with the idea. Fancy being able to move freely instead of being encased in a framework that makes you look like a hand-bell! And what a chance to show off the charms of a slim figure! Doña Elvira, needless to say, is all disapproval. She thinks the English style is indecent, and goes around muttering about "hussies looking as if they're wearing their night clothes." In her case, concealment is kind, but I don't see why those of us with less bulk to hide should go on being so restricted. Admittedly, it would be an immense amount of work to reshape all those skirts to hang properly without a hoop underneath, and we couldn't do it before the wedding. But afterwards – now, that's a different thing.

13th November 1501

Uncle Rod seems to take little pleasure in all the excitement and festivity. He shook his head this afternoon when I spoke to him about it, and said Queen Isabella would not approve of such gaudy extravagance. In her last letter to him, she remarked that money would be better spent in taking care of Catherine's long-term welfare – but that is not the Tudor way. Uncle Rod says their main aim is to impress the foreign royal families, because – and he glanced round to make sure nobody was listening – compared with those old ruling dynasties, the Tudors are an upstart lot with only a very slender claim to being royal at all. King Henry's mother, Lady Margaret Beaufort, is of royal stock, but on his father's side he comes of unruly Welsh landowners with a taste for fighting and good living. The crown was put on his head in all the blood and confusion of a battle fought at Bosworth Field, and they say it was retrieved from a thorn bush, where it had rolled from the head of the dead Richard III. Since then, Henry has tried throughout his reign to keep the peace, and he has succeeded in this – but his real battle is to win the respect of Europe's ancient royal families and he goes about that with the energy and determination of a soldier.

14th November 1501

The wedding. And what a day it's been! A whirlwind of colour and pageantry and feasting and wine – heavens, how these English drink! They are said to be the most truculent, law-resistant people in Europe, united among themselves only when fighting a common enemy, but their appetite for revelry is almost frightening. The King had caused the fountains to flow with burgundy wine after the marriage was celebrated, and the crowds were gulping it from their cupped hands, yelling and cheering, surging to and fro, careless of those who had fallen insensible and were being trampled over.

Catherine remained serene throughout it all. She looked lovely – as fresh and young as a girl making her First Communion – in her gown of white satin and with her long hair held by a circlet of gold and pearls. Those of us who had sat for so long stitching pierced seed pearls on to her veil with fine gold thread were rewarded when we saw her standing in that shimmer of delicate brightness. I wish Mama could have seen it – she would have been so proud.

Arthur, too, looked beautiful in his white clothes, and in the cathedral the pair of them stood out like two white swans against the deep, rich scarlet of the draperies and the massed gorgeousness of the courtiers. Margaret was gowned in cloth of gold as befits the future Queen of Scotland, and little Mary wore a dress of crimson velvet. Harry was in a richly embroidered tunic and a fur-trimmed cloak, and when the ceremony ended, it was he who escorted Catherine down the aisle to the waiting people massed outside. His face was proud and unsmiling, and I had the feeling that he was impatient with his youth, cursing it for casting him as the second son and not the elder.

We came in grand procession to Baynard's Castle, and feasted throughout the afternoon and evening. Gold platters gleamed in the light of hundreds of candles, and servants came in with course after course of soups and pies and roast meats (venison, rabbit, goose, swan and suckling pig) and then great cheeses and sweets (jellies and trifles and brandy-soaked cakes) – all served with an abundance of wine.

And then – I still blush a little when I think of this – the time came for the last part of the ceremony. Arthur and Catherine were escorted upstairs in a rather drunken procession headed by the Earl of Oxford.

There were several bishops as well, and boys swinging censers, and I don't know how many noblemen (most of them friends of Arthur's), laughing and making ribald jokes. Doña Elvira went as well, and so did I, together with Catherine's maid Maria and quite a lot of Spanish courtiers. I knew what was to happen. Doña Elvira had explained that it was a religious ceremony, and I watched while we all stood round the damask-curtained bed with the royal coat of arms embroidered at its head. The covers had been turned down to expose the undersheet and pillows, and amid the chanting of prayers, the Earl of Oxford laid himself down, first on Arthur's side of the bed then on Catherine's, and holy water was sprinkled on the bed. I thought it would make it dreadfully damp, but Doña Elvira was crossing herself fervently and so was everyone else, so I joined in. Arthur was being slapped on the back by his friends. His face looked very pale, and he took another long draught of wine, but one of the bishops frowned and removed the goblet from his hand, speaking to him in a stern whisper.

After that the crowd was shepherded out, though not without the shouting of some final bawdy jokes. I was not sure of their meaning – it's something men laugh about between themselves – but I felt terribly embarrassed for Catherine, who throughout all this had stood with clasped hands and lowered eyes. Doña Elvira kissed her and said she must be of good courage. Then she, too, went out. Maria and I stayed as Catherine had asked us, and we went into a small adjoining room to help her undress. Two men-servants were doing the same for Arthur.

Catherine was shivering although a fire burned in the bedroom.

We slipped the fine lawn nightdress over her head (I had banded it with Italian reticella work at the neck and sleeves) and Maria offered her a silk shawl to put about her shoulders. Catherine shook her head. Her hands were clasped at her mouth, and I could not tell whether she was praying or blowing on her fingers. "You must go now," she said. I hugged her, and could feel her body trembling, but she would never admit to being afraid.

I am writing this in the small room which I share with Maria, who is asleep. I wonder what has happened to Catherine this night. We used to giggle so often about the things grown-ups did when they went to bed together, but neither of us could do more than guess what they got up to. We knew it resulted in the birth of a baby, but exactly how the baby was started remained a mystery to us. When I was twelve and one day found I was bleeding, my mother gave me cloths to use and said it showed I was now a woman – but I didn't want to be a woman, I wanted to go on playing under the olive trees and having no cares.

Tomorrow, the mystery will be explained, for Catherine will surely tell me.

15th November 1501

I have learned nothing. Arthur came from the bedchamber late this morning, baggy-eyed and looking as any boy will look who has drunk far too much wine on the night before, but he managed to grin for his back-slapping friends. "This night I have been in the midst of Spain," he said, and they all cheered.

I went in to Catherine, who was still in bed. She looked very tired. I sat down beside her and took her hand, and she shrugged in answer to my unspoken question. "He snores," she said. "But he kissed me a lot." And that was all she told me. It's very disappointing.

24th November 1501

Uncle Rod was right about the Tudor determination to lay on a good show. The tournaments and jousting have been glorious to watch and the sumptuous banqueting has gone on and on. Every evening has been filled with music and dancing, and with astonishing theatrical events. Ingenious moving platforms brought in pageant after pageant – great structures peopled with choristers and actors, with gold and silver wolves that were really men and, amazingly, a ship in full sail that moved as though floating on water. Such artistry! And when the displays were over, musicians played for dancing. Catherine and I performed a Spanish seguidilla and everyone clapped and cheered us, then young Prince Harry danced with his sister Margaret. He is a great expert for one so young, quick and neat – but he was soon too hot in the many layers of his embroidered clothes (beautiful the way the fine-worked shirt sleeves are allowed to show through the slashed doublet), so he simply stripped off his overgown and tossed it aside, never breaking the rhythm as he danced on.

The last celebration was the best. After a banquet in the Parliament Chamber, they brought on what looked like a giant lantern as big as a bedchamber, with light glowing from inside its translucent panels – and within it were twelve beautiful ladies. It was as if we looked into a private fairyland. After this there arrived a towering, fantastic chapel of many layers and compartments, with children singing at its upper windows while doors below opened to release a whole colony of baby rabbits that ran everywhere. Then eight ladies appeared at other doors in the intricately painted structure, and opened basketfuls of white doves that flew round the vast hall and settled on the high beams above us. Glorious, glorious.

But yesterday the festivities ended, and the Spanish nobles and their ladies who came only for the wedding are preparing to leave. Everything seems very flat.

26th November 1501

The King had one more trick up his sleeve. This morning he asked Catherine and her ladies to come to his library, and while he was showing us the books with their beautifully painted pictures and their tooled and gilded covers, a man suddenly came out from behind the shelves, holding a great casket. He opened it at the King's instruction, and we all gasped, for it was full of magnificent jewellery – diamonds, sapphires, rubies and emeralds set into necklaces, coronets, rings, brooches and bracelets, all with intricate gold and silver work. The King told Catherine to take what she wanted, and she dipped her hand into the sparkling mass, lifting out one beautiful thing after another and exclaiming with delight at each one.

When she had made her choices, King Henry turned to us and said we, too, might select a gift. Doña Elvira took a large brooch set with rubies and garnets, and Maria had a delicate necklace of pearls and filigree silver. And I have an opal ring. The stone seems to glow with fire and blue sky, and it is the most wonderful thing I have ever owned.

29th November 1501

A bustle of packing is going on, for the court is soon to move from Baynard's Castle to Windsor. Catherine and what remains of her Spanish entourage will not be going with them. We are to move to a manor owned by Prince Arthur in a place called Bewdley, in Worcestershire.

There has been much debate, Uncle Rod confided to me, about whether Catherine and Arthur are old enough to live yet as man and wife. I couldn't see why not – what is the point of being married if your lives are not shared? But he looked reserved, as he often does, and reminded me that Catherine's brother, Juan, had died in the early months of his marriage to the Princess of Portugal – a terrible tragedy for Isabella and Ferdinand to lose their only son. The doctors thought, he said, that his death might have been caused by over-exertion. I do not see why marriage should be considered an exertion. At worst, it seems likely to be merely tiresome.

10th December 1501

There is hardly room for us all in this house, a cold place although Arthur has had glass put in the windows. We will move again to Ludlow Castle, on the borders of Wales, they say.

I am hurrying to finish embroidering a kerchief for Catherine's birthday in six days' time. It is a design of two birds and a twining of vine leaves, done in our Spanish blackwork, a style much admired here by the English ladies.

The weather is turning very cold.

15th January 1502

Today, Margaret will be officially betrothed to James IV of Scotland, though we will not be there to see it. Everyone says we are not missing much – a betrothal is not the same as a full-blown wedding – but any diversion would be welcome. This castle is dank and forbidding, and the misted mountains of Wales loom in a constant shroud of rain.

The procedures of royal weddings are very strange. Tomorrow there will be a proxy marriage, which is not the real thing but an exchange of vows made by stand-ins. Uncle Rod stood in for Catherine at her proxy wedding years ago, and I can't imagine anyone who looks less like a bride. Or even, for that matter, like a groom. Poor Uncle Rod – his wife died when Gonsalvo was born, and he has never replaced her, or even seemed to want to.

The court ladies here eye Catherine constantly – looking, I suppose, for that swelling of the waistline which means a baby is on its way. She remains as slim as ever, and spends much of her time praying in the strange, circular chapel (where every sound echoes in such a ghostly way). Praying for what? For a child, perhaps. Every royal family prays earnestly and constantly for sons, so that a supply of future kings may never be in doubt.

Maria whispers to me that in Arthur and Catherine's case there is doubt. One of the English chambermaids told her there was no blood on the royal sheets after their wedding night, and it seems there should have been if, as the woman put it, "they was properly married". This, too, I do not understand. Maria suggests that we are just the same as dogs and cats and horses – but surely human beings must be different? But the more I think of it, the more I fear she may be right.

There are alarming rumours about the Scottish king. If we do indeed behave like dogs, then he is a very active one, running after every bitch in sight. He has several children already, it is said, by different women whom he has loved but not married, and yet by all accounts he is a civilized man, scholarly and thoughtful, fond of music and art and keenly interested in science. According to Don Pedro de Ayala, he possesses instruments for the pulling out of teeth, but if he is called on to do this he pays the patient for the pain he has caused. He sounds a strange man, but an interesting one.

Uncle Rod says James did not really want to marry Margaret because he was deeply devoted to a woman called Margaret Drummond and refused to give her up. The court advisers were at their wits' end – and then Mistress Drummond conveniently died. It was poison, they say. Her two sisters who shared that final meal with her died also. I was appalled when I heard this. I asked Uncle Rod who had done it, but he shook his head. There are some things it is better not to know, he said.

15th February 1502

How long will this winter go on? I am sick with longing for Spain, where the sun shines even in these short days, and at night there is a blaze of stars. Here there is nothing but clouds and greyness and mud and the smell of wet stone. The Spanish courtiers share my discontent, and the only man here with any sense of purpose is Don Alessandro Geraldini, who taught Catherine and me when we were children and is now the priest who hears our confession. He at least is busy, trying to reassure us that we are not forgotten by God in this gloomy place.

27th March 1502

Catherine is ill. It began with a shivering fit that worsened by the hour, and now she lies half-insensible, on fire with fever yet pouring with perspiration. People here call it the sweating sickness. Their main concern is for Arthur, from whom Catherine caught the illness. He seems gravely ill, and although the doctors have bled him, he gets no better.

Doña Elvira says we should keep to our own rooms for fear of contagion, but Catherine calls for me in her delirium and how could I refuse to go to her? I sponge her face and body with warm water and dry her with a soft towel, but there is little else I can do except sit beside her so that she knows I am there. God protect her.

3rd April 1502

Prince Arthur died yesterday. A rider has been sent to London, to tell the King. I cannot write much. The fever caught me in turn and I am very weak.

20th April 1502

Catherine is alive, though she is still not well. Arthur lies in his coffin in the round chapel, and the air is heavy with the smell of herbs used by the embalmer. They will take him from here in three days' time to be buried in Worcester Cathedral.

I still feel shaky and exhausted. My back aches and my fingers are sore from hours of sewing. Countless bales of black silk have had to be cut and stitched into mourning dress for all the people here. Seven courtiers have died of the sickness, and I do not know how many servants.

4th May 1502

They are back now from the long business of the funeral. We watched the procession leave the castle ten days ago in torrential rain. Two Spanish noblemen rode at its head to represent Catherine, for she is too weak and ill to leave the castle. The coffin on its bier was pulled by four horses that laboured and steamed in the deep mud, and the men who splashed alongside had a hard job to keep the black canopy above it in place, stumbling and slipping as they were.

It got worse along the way, they tell me. The horses had to be replaced by oxen, whose powerful bodies and split hooves get a better grip. How shameful, though, that the corpse of gentle Prince Arthur should be hauled through the mire by beasts of the field.

Don Alessandro was with them. The rain stopped, he says, when they got to Worcester, so at least they could approach the cathedral with fresh black horses and some semblance of dignity. The assembled bishops looked magnificent, he said. I wish I had been there to see them. The English embroidery done for the church is famous all over Europe – the opus Anglicanum, it is called. I saw something of it at Catherine's wedding, but the robes worn for a funeral would be different, rich and dark.

Even at this time of grief, the Tudor gift of theatricality did not desert them. The coffin was covered in cloth of gold, and each nobleman who came in added his own golden pall, so that the dead prince lay under a mound of gleaming softness. A man of arms rode a black horse down the aisle of the cathedral, bearing Arthur's armour and his battle-axe, its head to the floor, and the court officials who carried golden staffs of office broke them in two and cast the pieces into the grave.

Catherine is beginning to regain her strength, but she seems lost and confused. At sixteen, she is a widow. The courtiers still cling to a faint hope that she may be carrying Arthur's child, but Doña Elvira shakes her head firmly at any mention of it. Catherine herself says nothing.

17th June 1502

At last the weather is dry. It is so good to go out of doors without the hems of one's dress becoming fouled with mud and one's shoes sodden. Catherine has had a letter from her mother, who has only just heard of Prince Arthur's death. Queen Isabella wants Catherine to come home to Spain. She says Ludlow Castle is an unhealthy place, and her daughter must leave it at once. A flutter of hope ran through all the Spaniards here, for all of us long for the sun and for warm tiles under our feet instead of these stinking rushes – but Catherine will not go. Her mouth is set in the obstinate line I know so well, and nothing will move her. The English must keep their side of the bargain, she says. She came here out of duty to marry Prince Arthur, on the promise that she would receive one third of the income from Wales, Chester and Cornwall. "They will not shuffle me off so easily," she says. And means it.

24th June 1502

One battle, at least, has been won. We are to move to London next week.

25th July 1502

We are at Durham House in the Strand, a road which runs by the River Thames in London. It's a grand house, built for the bishops of Durham but used mostly by visiting ambassadors. There's a garden laid out in the Italian style, with low hedges of clipped yew and rosemary, and high walls on either side with peach and plum trees trained against them. Stairs lead down to the river, where one may step into a boat to be rowed up to Westminster – far pleasanter than being jolted over the cobbles in a carriage.

Inside, there's a great hall, as there has been in all the other mansion houses I've seen, with a gallery at one end where musicians can play. This is summer, so it's not so cold, but smoke drifts past the carved screen from the kitchen and its fires, all part of the same room.

I'd hoped London streets would be cleaner than the muddy lanes of Wales, but there seems to be little difference. The paving hardly exists, and to make things worse, great troupes of oxen go through with barrels of water on their backs, churning up the mud and adding to it with their droppings. In the heavy warmth of the English summer the stink is dreadful.

Uncle Rod was here yesterday on official business. He brought the new envoy from Spain, a tall man called Hernan, the Duke of Estrada. They went to a long meeting from which Doña Elvira emerged looking flushed and angry, and I was longing to know what had happened. I caught my uncle in the garden for a few moments, and he told me there is a huge argument going on about Catherine's dowry. King Ferdinand paid the first half of it – 100,000 crowns – at the time of the wedding, but he now refuses to pay the second half. His daughter no longer has a husband, he says, so the English cannot claim that their side of the bargain has been kept. What's more, he wants the first half returned.

King Henry is furious, of course. He was counting on the money from Spain, and if he doesn't get it, he will not give Catherine her promised income. Indeed, he has not done so up until now, which is why none of her Spanish attendants has yet been paid. I told Uncle Rod how discontented we all feel, and asked if he could persuade the King to release just a little of the money, but he pursed his lips and shook his head. It would be indelicate to speak of money just now, he said, when the King and Queen are still in mourning for their son. I suppose diplomats have to learn to be patient.

26th July 1502

A letter has come from my mother. She has written only once before, in answer to my letter, and then she was full of concern for my welfare, but this time she mentions larger things. King Louis of France has invaded Italy, and there is a danger that Spain will be surrounded by hostile French forces. The English must stand by us, Mama says. Can't Uncle Rod start negotiating for a new marriage between Catherine and the King's younger son, Harry?

She doesn't realize that young Harry is still only eleven years old. A boy is not of legal age to marry until he is fourteen, so there are three years to wait. I think Catherine wishes it were otherwise, for there is something about Harry's broad-shouldered stance and direct, ruthless stare that disturbs every female heart, young though he is.

1st August 1502

The Spanish retainers here are growing louder in their complaints. They had hoped that Estrada was going to persuade the King to release some money so they would be paid, but nothing has happened and we are all penniless, Catherine as well. Fewer candles burn in the big iron holders, and the cooks present us with thin soup and tough meat, and their faces are full of contempt. Uncle Rod warns me to be careful what I say, but he explained privately that the King's prime concern is not with Catherine or Spain, but to bring about the wedding between Margaret and King James of Scotland. He needs this strong link, because he is always afraid that the Scots, who have no great love for England, will side with France. Margaret and James would have been married by now had it not been for Arthur's death and the mourning that followed it, and Henry is full of plans for sending his daughter on the long journey to Edinburgh, with all the great train of soldiers, attendants and courtiers who must go with her. So we will have to wait.

2nd August 1502

Today Doña Elvira flounced into the sewing room and flopped down so heavily that she sent scraps of silk flying everywhere, and burst into tears. Maria and I patted and consoled her, asking what was the matter, and she blurted out indignantly that she had only tried to be helpful. At a meeting with the King and my uncle and various dignitaries, she had said there was no reason why Catherine should not marry Henry's younger son, because her marriage to Arthur had not been "a proper one".

She was so agitated that she found herself blurting out what nobody has ever told me. It seems we do indeed copulate in the same way as animals, but when this happens to a girl for the first time, it causes her to bleed a little. In Catherine and Arthur's case, this did not happen, Doña Elvira says. She would have known, and so would the servants who changed the bed linen.

Apparently this makes a legal difference to Catherine's status. If her marriage to Arthur was not "consummated", as they call it, then it has no standing in law. Catherine remains a virgin – and this, Doña Elvira says, is a good thing because there is a passage in the Bible which forbids a man to marry his brother's widow. If Catherine really was

Arthur's proper wife, then she could not marry his brother. Spain and England need a second marriage, so why are they not glad to know it is perfectly possible? She burst into noisy tears all over again, deeply offended that she had been told to be quiet and that she could not know what she was talking about.

I ran across to Uncle Rod's lodgings in the Strand this evening – a poor place, but he, too, has not been paid for months – and asked him to explain. Doña Elvira had put her foot in it rather badly, it seems, though she didn't know the other side of it. If Catherine was indeed not Arthur's "proper wife", then she has no right to the title of Princess of Wales, and no claim to be supported by King Henry. She cannot call herself a royal widow, because she was never a royal wife. She is nothing.

What a nightmare! We are caught in the middle of a dispute between kings, and either way, Catherine is the loser. I wish she would abandon this hopeless struggle, and go home. But she won't.

10th August 1502

The King's wife, Queen Elizabeth, has given Catherine some money. It's not a lot, Catherine confided as we sat stitching by the open window this afternoon, but at least she can pay her servants something of what they are owed. She glanced round to make sure the door was shut, then leaned towards me and said, "Do you know how she got it? She pawned some of the gold plate! Just fancy!"

I'm sure the King does not know. He lives with penny-pinching meanness, counting each candle and refusing to have a fire in his room even though he suffers from asthma and coughs constantly. How many candles will he have to save to pay for sending his daughter in splendour to marry the Scottish king? But as my uncle points out, Henry's concerns about Scotland come first at the moment. "I will keep trying, my dear," he said. "After all, I am a Spaniard. All my sympathies are with Catherine. But I have to be careful." No wonder he looks so tired sometimes.

23rd August 1502

Thomas Fish was here today, bringing Catherine some linen cloth and a length of fine lawn for a pair of embroidered sleeves. He had just come from Windsor, where he takes cloth regularly for the Queen. He also took her some cherry jam made by his wife, for Queen Elizabeth is pregnant again, and has a great longing for the sharp taste of cherries. She has a pet monkey, he says, and this morning it tore to shreds a notebook in which the King keeps his private accounts. His roars of rage made the whole palace tremble, Fish said, and the monkey leapt to Elizabeth for protection. It would be safe with her, for she is a kind woman. Everyone prays she will have a healthy son to replace the lost Arthur. According to Fish, she told her grieving husband, "We are both young enough."

11th February 1503

The Queen has given birth to a daughter. There is rejoicing, of course, but of a slightly muted kind. A son would have been so much better. The little girl is to be called Katherine, spelled the English way, and all the Spaniards here are pleased.

13th February 1503

Queen Elizabeth is ill with the child-bed fever. We all went to Mass to pray for her safe recovery, but the smell of incense reminded me of the heavy scent that hung about Ludlow after Arthur had died. I must put such thoughts away, for fear they may come true.

20th February 1503

Our prayers did not save her. Sweet Elizabeth, Queen of England, died today on her 37th birthday. We are plunged again into mourning, and the baby Katherine is sickly and unlikely to live. Rain falls like tears.

4th March 1503

All London is in mourning. The state funeral of the Queen took place today at Westminster Abbey, and the chief mourner was Lady Katherine Courtney, after whom the baby, now also dead, had been called. So much for our Spanish hopes that it had been Catherine who was thus honoured.

It was beautifully done, of course. All along Cheapside, groups of 37 white-clad young girls, one for each year of the Queen's life, stood holding lit tapers, their heads wreathed in leaves and white flowers. Green and white, the Tudor colours. Candles burned in every parish church and torches flared in the sunless London streets, lighting the Queen to her rest.

Only a few weeks ago, anticipating the end of the year's mourning for Arthur, the Queen gave her daughter Margaret a magnificent gown of crimson, trimmed with the black squirrel fur they call pampilyon. Poor Margaret. Once again her marriage is postponed, and now she must face the journey to Scotland, when it comes, without the support of her beloved mother. She is a happy girl, given the chance, and these months of wearing black have damped her gay spirits. She was so glad when half-mourning allowed her to put a pair of embroidered white sleeves to her black dress, and then bright ones of orange sarcenet, which she loved. There was such a fuss in September when the court removed from Baynard's Castle to Westminster and she found that the orange sleeves had been left behind. Richard Justice, the Queen's Page of the Robes, was sent back to fetch them in a hired boat, which he was pleased about because he got paid extra. But now Margaret is in deepest black again, and her marriage will not take place until the summer.

6th March 1503

I found Catherine sitting by the window this morning, staring out at the river in something close to despair. She told me King Henry is thinking of marrying her himself now that Elizabeth is dead. Trying to cheer her up, I said, "But at least that way you would be the Queen of England" – but we both knew how hollow the words were.

Catherine looked at me very straight. "That's the wrong way, Eva," she said. "I *will* be queen one day, but not through marrying Henry. He is 46 and I am seventeen. With his bad chest and his gout, he might die within a couple of years, and then where would I be? A dowager whom nobody wants. Even if I bore his child, it would not be heir to the throne, for that position is Harry's. So I must be Harry's wife, not his father's."

She is right, of course, but it seems an impossible hope. Three years to wait before the royal boy is old enough to marry, and even then, she may not be the one they choose.

26th March 1503

The King's mother, Lady Margaret Beaufort, has come to Windsor to take over the running of the royal household. She is immensely capable – I remember well those magnificent banquets at the time of Catherine's wedding, all of which were organized by her.

Catherine is looking happier. A letter from Queen Isabella has dealt very firmly with Henry's idea of marrying her daughter. A barbarous notion, she told him. She suggests he should consider the widowed Queen of Naples, who would be much more suitable. Henry, apparently, is sending an envoy out there to inspect her and report back.

5th June 1503

At last Margaret has started on her journey to Scotland for her wedding with James. Henry has gone with her and all her retinue to his mother's mansion in Collyweston, the first step on the way, and they will all stay there for some days, hunting and disporting themselves. Margaret looked happy at last. She rode a white palfrey whose saddlecloth was embroidered with red roses and the lion of Scotland, and a litter fringed in gold followed her so that she could rest and be carried if she tired of riding. The whole train looked magnificent with its banners flying and the baggage carts striped in white and green, and crowds lined the streets to cheer her. The journey will take a month and the wedding is set for 8th August.

Meanwhile, our living conditions get worse. The bread is dark, musty-tasting stuff, made from bad flour that has started to ferment, and I suspect that mice have got at it, too. My stocks of thread and fabric are almost all used up, and I hate to think of the shameful inactivity that will follow when they are gone. Stripped of any pride in my skilled work, I will be reduced to a mere pauper, living on the crumbs of charity. I have not started on a new design for several weeks, and use my remaining silks for the careful mending of our clothes. As to my function as an interpreter, it is never called for now, although Catherine's grasp of English is not good. No English courtier has any need to speak to her. We are utterly forgotten.

23rd June 1503

Great news! Uncle Rod's patient diplomacy has succeeded at last – or something has – for a treaty of intended marriage between Harry and Catherine has been signed. There was such a spontaneous lifting of spirits among us that we needed to celebrate, so off we went down the river to Hampton Court, where Henry is building a great palace. Some of the English nobles came with us, for now they notice again that we exist, and several of them brought their dogs and crossbows and falcons for an afternoon's hunting in the countryside. The hawks wore little hoods when they were not flying – as ours do in Spain – but the stitchery of jewels and silver wire on these hoods was exquisite, making the birds look like little emperors as they sat in their darkness.

How strange the English are. In some ways they seem brutish and crude, full of uncouth vulgarity, and yet one hears music sung and played everywhere, and their clothes and linens are a glory of fine, colourful work. They seem to take a lusty joy in beauty of all kinds, and for this one can forgive them much.

5th October 1503

The King has granted Catherine an allowance of 100 pounds a month. She says it will not go far towards keeping us all and paying off her debts (and she wants to retrieve some of the plate she was forced to pawn), but it is much better than nothing.

Nobody gives Uncle Rod any credit for his part in this, though I know it was his work that brought it about. Doña Elvira treats him with open contempt, even though he spoke to the King on her behalf when the Spanish retainers were particularly unruly and caused him to give her a cloth-of-gold cap as a sign of his trust in her authority.

I know what lies behind the courtiers' lack of generosity towards my uncle, though nobody will voice it aloud – at least, not to me. They all know Rodrigo De Puebla is – or was – Jewish, though he converted to Christianity, as did the whole family. We didn't have much choice. Eleven years ago, Queen Isabella exiled all Jews, because for her, the Christian crusade is everything. My last letter from Mama says the Queen has permitted an Inquisition to be set up, testing the true faith of anyone about whom there is a shadow of doubt. There are rumours, she says, that its officers do not shrink from the use of terrible tortures or even death. For the first time, I am almost glad to be away from my country. My uncle and I never speak of the blood tie that binds us to a persecuted people – it is safer not to. But I see in his face sometimes a great weariness, and understand it.

Catherine, alas, has no understanding of my uncle's slow, careful work. She is impatient by nature, and much preferred Don Pedro Ayala of the wink and the charming smile – but he has been recalled to Spain.

8th November 1503

Fog shrouds the garden and hangs heavy over the river. There is no joy in going out, and the house is full of bickering and whispers. The question of whether Catherine's marriage to Arthur was a proper one is still being wrangled over, and my uncle says they are waiting for the Pope to give a judgement.

On another matter, though, my uncle has had a great success. He has brought about an agreement that English merchants trading in Spain will have all the rights and privileges of Spaniards, paying no extra charges and being free to load their cargoes without taxation. The same is true for Spaniards trading in England. I, at least, am very proud of him.

27th November 1503

The court has shifted its quarters from Windsor to Richmond. They move several times a year, lucky things, leaving the previous palace to be cleaned of soot and stripped of its vilely muddy and stinking rushes. I must say, much of the filth and stink in the houses is the fault of their occupants. If the men would refrain from pissing in the fireplaces, it would help. We Spaniards are not included in the "progress", as they call it, of the King and his court from one place to another, and Durham House is becoming disgusting.

18th February 1504

A young English lord wants to marry Maria de Rochas. He is the grandson of the Earl of Derby, very handsome in the fair, English way, and Maria is much in love with him. She went to Catherine to ask her blessing on the match, and to raise the question of a dowry. As one of Catherine's ladies, she should have dowry money provided by the royal purse – but Catherine has no funds to meet a request of this size. She has written to her father about it, but there is silence.

1st March 1504

Still no response from King Ferdinand on the question of Maria's dowry. She is beginning to fear that her suitor will look elsewhere.

9th March 1504

Poor Maria. Young Derby has withdrawn his offer, and she is utterly cast down. To make matters worse, Doña Elvira went to her and said she was glad the "silly affair" was over, for she wants Maria for her own son, Iñigo Manrique, master of the king's pages.

Catherine is furious. She suspects that Doña Elvira intercepted her letters to Ferdinand and made sure they were never sent. There was a tremendous quarrel this morning, and Catherine has told my uncle he must do something about replacing Doña Elvira. Uncle Rod looked helpless and pointed out that Queen Isabella has every faith in the duenna, who is charged to act as mother-substitute to Catherine while she is in England. Catherine retorted that she has no need of a mother-substitute. At eighteen, she is old enough to run her own affairs, and if she wants to get rid of Doña Elvira she should be able to do so. Doña Elvira remarked to her husband – but loud enough to be overheard – that it would take more than a jumped-up little Jewish go-between to remove her from her post. There are times when I hate her.

12th December 1504

Terrible news. We have just heard that Queen Isabella died two weeks ago, on November 26th. Catherine is huddled in her bed, weeping, and the courtiers stand in hushed groups, talking in low voices about what is to happen now. My uncle has gone to Windsor, to consult with the King.

If only Catherine's brother were still alive. So many problems would be solved were he here to step into his mother's shoes. Ferdinand has no claim in his own right, though as Isabella's widower he will fight hard to retain his kingship. Officially, the throne must go to Juana, Catherine's oldest sister – but she is married to Prince Philip of the Netherlands, and lives with him and their children in that flat, damp country which, people tell me, is even duller than England. It's a long way from Spain, and Dutch Philip will seem a strange king on the Spanish throne.

I wonder what Juana is like now. It's years since I have seen her. She was always very beautiful, as dark-eyed and graceful as a deer, and as easily startled. She fell deeply in love with Philip at first sight. Catherine used to read out her letters in those early days, and we would giggle over the passion they expressed. We were only young, and I suppose we found it a bit embarrassing. Does Juana still feel the same about him, I wonder? It is rumoured that Philip is constantly unfaithful to her. One of the English ladies smiled and said, "You know they call her Juana the Mad?" I hope it is not true.

16th December 1504

A letter came from Mama today. She speaks of the Queen's death, naturally. And she says Juana's nerves have been badly affected by her husband's infidelities – or so the gossip goes in Spain. Poor Juana. Has her husband really driven her mad?

Uncle Rod shrugged wearily when I spoke to him about it. Neither Philip nor Ferdinand want Juana to be thought sane, he says, because she in fact is the one who inherits the throne, and the big quarrel is between her father and her husband, both of whom want to rule in her place.

I so much hope for Catherine's sake that Ferdinand will manage to go on being king. It has been a terrible blow to her to lose her mother, and if her father is pushed out by Philip, it will be the end of all Catherine's hopes of a match with Harry. Her only value is in being the daughter of the Spanish king, and if that is lost, then so is everything else. But Philip is very powerful. His father, Maximilian, is Emperor of all the German states and of Austria, Flanders and Burgundy, a man of ruthless ambition, backed by all the authority of his aristocratic Habsburg family. I fear the worst, though I will not say so to Catherine.

Sometimes I wish I had someone else to talk to. Not just Uncle Rod, wise and kind though he is, but a friend my own age who would share my worries. Someone strong and dependable, a man-friend, I suppose I mean. Things are hard here, and getting harder. Catherine insists on using most of her allowance to reclaim her valuables, saying they are her only security for the future, but this means we are still half-destitute. We live on little but bread now, and on gristly bits of meat that we would have thrown to the dogs when we first came here. I can't afford to get my shoes mended, so my feet are constantly cold, and water-sodden if I try to venture out. But I must not complain to Catherine. Most of the Spaniards here are angry with her, and she has enough to bear.

7th May 1505

King Ferdinand has taken a new wife. She is Germaine of Foix – a French woman. The court is buzzing with indignation. One or two of the more thoughtful ones say it could be a clever move, designed to placate the French king and prevent him from attacking Spain, but most people simply think he is siding with Spain's enemy. That's what King Henry thinks, quite obviously. Thomas Fish was here again today, having come from Richmond with new supplies of linens and thread (thank God!), and he said Henry was raging, calling Ferdinand a turncoat and a traitor.

Catherine, too, is angry, but not with her father, whom she trusts absolutely. She is sure that the marriage with Germaine is a means to win a breathing space from the French threat, and she berates our Spanish courtiers for not believing this. I don't know where she gets her energy and determination from. I do my best to feel as she does, but the effort leaves me tired and filled with secret doubts.

19th May 1505

Roger Fellowes has been paying me a lot of attention, and Catherine says he is in love with me. I do hope not. He has ginger hair and very pale eyelashes, and he blushes whenever he sees me. He comes of a good family and is very polite, but his is not the shoulder I would ever bury my face on. I cannot take seriously a man who looks like a peeled shrimp.

27th June 1505

Our fears were well founded. Prince Harry has backed out of the marriage agreement, though rumour has it that he looks guilty and wretched, and he was talked into it by the King and his close adviser, a man called Thomas Wolsey. The excuse is that Harry was under legal age when he made the agreement, so it is not binding, but it's quite obvious that his father has decided to seek a better match for his son and heir than Catherine.

Harry will be fourteen tomorrow. In law he will be a man; and he looks a man, taller than most even now, and broad and strong. I had let myself dream that Catherine would marry him on this day, but all those hopes are ruined now. Harry himself has probably had no say in it. For the last year or more, his father has kept him tightly secluded, shut in a small room beyond the King's own chamber, and all the reports we have of the boy say he looks sulky and resentful, far from his old gaiety.

Catherine has said nothing about the new announcement. Her face is pale, but her mouth is firmly set and her fierce look deters anyone from mentioning it. This evening, as we struggled to find something edible on a couple of herrings that had been far too long out of the sea, she said to me quietly, "Harry and I *will* be married, Eva. But first the old king will have to die." I suppose the words shocked me, for she smiled as she broke off a piece of bread and glanced round to make sure nobody else had heard. "Time is on my side," she said. "You'll see."

20th September 1505

The Spanish have abandoned the trade treaty my uncle brought about, and the effect is disastrous. Eight hundred merchants have just come back from Spain, complaining that they have been ruined by the extortionate prices asked by the Spaniards, and demanding that Henry do something about it. So Henry shouted at Uncle Rod, blaming him for the treaty's collapse. He could be heard all through the court, it is said, bellowing that De Puebla had betrayed him. So unfair.

22nd September 1505

In his fury with all things Spanish, the King has withdrawn Catherine's allowance, and she is in despair. How is she to run this house and feed all these people, no matter how meanly, on no money whatsoever? Durham House is a wretched place now, the linen soiled and torn and the stink of half-rotten fish and meat mingling with the general reek of sodden rushes and filth.

Doña Elvira goes round saying that King Ferdinand obviously knows nothing of our plight, otherwise he would do something about it. She blames poor Uncle Rod, whom she calls "that little rat" for having kept Ferdinand in the dark. My uncle protests that he is in constant contact with the Spanish king and has repeatedly told him of the situation, but Doña Elvira sweeps past him with her nose in the air. She is constantly cooing over Catherine and reminding her of how badly we are all treated, but she bullies everyone else. Poor Maria de Rochas has had to agree to marry Doña Elvira's stuck-up son, because her English admirer stopped admiring her when she became as poor and shabby as the rest of us.

23rd September 1505

Doña Elvira has suggested that Catherine should meet with her sister, Juana. The region of Calais in France still belongs to England, and they could meet there, she says, a convenient halfway point between London and the Netherlands. Once Juana understands how miserable her sister is, she will tell their father, and something will be done about it.

Catherine is very excited by the idea. I can see why – she is lonely here, and it's a long time since she saw her sister. And, to my sadness, she believes Doña Elvira's story that my uncle is not telling Ferdinand of her plight.

Doña Elvira says the meeting will be simple. Her brother, Don Juan Manuel, is the Spanish ambassador at the court of Emperor Maximilian, so he knows Philip well and will organize everything. The pair of them plan that King Henry himself will go with Catherine, and Philip will escort Juana – it will be a splendid meeting. Catherine agrees, and she has written a letter to Philip, putting the suggestion to him. And I told Uncle Rod.

29th September 1505

A reply from Philip has come back very quickly, and Catherine seems delighted.

30th September 1505

Heavens, what drama! My uncle was here this morning and, as we stood talking, Catherine came up with Philip's letter, as well as one she had just written to Henry, asking him if he will go with her to the meeting. Uncle Rod looked appalled, but he is always diplomatic. He suggested politely that Catherine should hand over both letters to him and let him do the negotiations – but Catherine would have none of that. Her chin was in the air in that obstinate way I know so well, and she told my uncle she was quite capable of managing her own affairs, and if he had anything to say about it, he had better speak to Doña Elvira. So off she went with the letters, leaving Uncle Rod to brave the dragon.

I caught him later, and he said Doña Elvira had promised to make sure the letter to the King was not sent. "Don't you see?" he said. "It will cause the final rift with Ferdinand if Henry goes off to a private meeting with Philip – a diplomatic disaster." He didn't trust Doña Elvira, feeling pretty sure she would send the letter all the same. He went back to his lodgings because his landlady would have his supper ready, but he left his servant at Durham House, to watch what happened.

After that, the fun really started. The servant saw Doña Elvira give the letter to a man who rode off into the night, and rushed across to tell Uncle Rod, who came hobbling as fast as his gouty legs would carry him to tackle Catherine about it. I've never seen him so upset – he was actually in tears – but then, of course, he was looking at the ruin of all his careful work to keep good relations between England and Spain.

For once, Catherine listened. I watched her face darken as she heard how Doña Elvira had for years been sending court secrets to her brother, where they were fed straight to Philip and Maximilian. For all the flattering talk about King Ferdinand, she had in fact been working against him. She and her brother wanted to see Philip on the throne of Spain, and the proposed meeting of royal sisters was simply a way to bring Henry into personal contact with Philip, perhaps leading to a pact between them to launch a joint attack on Ferdinand. No wonder Uncle Rod was so upset!

It was too late to stop Catherine's letter from reaching the King, but my uncle explained to her that if the meeting went ahead, it might result in her father's exile or even his death.

He didn't have to explain any further. Catherine sat down at her desk and dipped a pen into the inkwell. "Tell me what I must write," she said. And at Uncle Rod's dictation, she put down an apology for not having understood the situation, and begged the King's pardon for having suggested a meeting which he might have found embarrassing. Then she went to see Doña Elvira.

We all know Catherine has a temper, but I have never heard such an outburst of fury as the one which followed. She berated the duenna at a pitch that could be heard all over the house, and we listened in guilty delight to the goings-on. Whenever Doña Elvira tried to say anything, the torrent of words got faster and louder, until the dusty tapestries on the walls seemed to quiver with Catherine's rage. When Doña Elvira at last came out, her face was crimson and her mouth set like a trap. She met nobody's eye but went to her bedroom and slammed the door.

23rd October 1505

Doña Elvira left this morning, saying she needs to consult a doctor in the Netherlands about her eyes, though we have never heard her complain of poor sight. She has taken her husband, her son and the unfortunate Maria, and nobody expects to see them back.

6th November 1505

Everything is changing. After Doña Elvira left, Catherine went to King Henry and said she was now alone in running Durham House and she really must have some money.

It was a mistake. When Henry heard of the duenna's departure, he said Catherine could not possibly remain unchaperoned and in charge of such a big household. Fifty Spanish retainers was an unreasonable number anyway. Most of them could be sent home and Catherine could move into court with a small staff.

There was a huge argument about who should go back to Spain and who should stay, followed by a commotion of packing, and tomorrow those of us who remain will go to Richmond Palace for the winter. Somehow, I regret leaving Durham House, squalid though it has become. It has been our own place, and now we will have no proper home, only what rooms the English choose to give us in their various grand houses. Catherine does not complain – she says the move may be useful. I know what she means – she will be nearer to Prince Harry and to the centre of whatever is going on. But I am leaving Uncle Rod behind in his shabby lodgings, and I feel bereft.

13th January 1506

Great excitement has seized the court. Philip of the Netherlands and Juana, with an enormous entourage in a great fleet of ships, were caught in a storm while sailing to Spain to claim the throne from Ferdinand, and they have been blown ashore in England. They are at a place called Melcombe Regis in Dorset, amid the wreckage of their fleet. Several ships were sunk and the surviving ones are battered and broken. Philip sent a rider to London, to tell Henry of his plight, so a train of baggage-waggons and horses and carriages has been despatched for their rescue, and here we are in a ferment of preparation to receive the royal guests.

How ironic that the meeting which Doña Elvira failed to bring about has been achieved after all, by foul weather! My uncle is in constant consultation with the King, planning what advantage can be seized from this opportunity. Weather, he explained to me, is neutral. There is nothing clandestine about this meeting – it is pure chance, and nobody can accuse Henry of plotting. But the situation in Spain remains very delicate, with Ferdinand moving ever closer to an understanding with France. He has signed a treaty with Louis XII which, among other things, prevents Philip and Juana from setting foot on French soil, which is why they had to make their journey to Spain by sea. It may be, Uncle Rod says sadly, that Henry will have to seek Philip's friendship now rather than Ferdinand's – but he still hopes to prevent an all-out attack on Catherine's father.

Catherine herself is suddenly the centre of attention again. Since moving into Richmond we have been treated like poor relations, housed in mean little rooms and openly despised, but now, as Juana's sister, Catherine must be made presentable. We have been given some silk to make her a new gown, and a frenzy of cutting and stitching is going on.

29th January 1506

A second herald arrived from Philip this morning, to say the procession from Dorset is near London now, and should arrive tomorrow. To Catherine's disappointment, Juana is not with them – the near-shipwreck and the drowning of so many people has upset her so greatly that she is unfit to travel.

31st January 1506

They are here! There seemed no end to the pouring in of horses and carriages, nobles, attendants and soldiers – huge numbers of soldiers. Evidently Philip has every intention of routing Ferdinand by force if necessary. Lady Margaret, the King's mother, has made her preparations wonderfully well, and has coped with the great invasion smoothly. She has sent the soldiers off to Croydon, where they will be housed in the Archbishop of Canterbury's palace in far more comfort than they are used to.

Philip himself was ushered into the royal rooms that are hung with tapestries and cloth of gold, and he could not help being impressed when he saw the chamber where he is to sleep. He guessed correctly that it must be Henry's own room, the walls swathed in crimson velvet caught between embroidered bosses depicting the royal coat of arms, but Henry gave a casual shrug and said it was merely a guest room. Nobody smiled, though we all knew how much frantic stitching and decorating has gone on. The King has moved into the rather bleak emptiness of Queen Elizabeth's rooms, closed and unused since her death.

Now we are set for days of jousting and tournament and nights of revelry. Harry's little sister, Mary, is ten years old now, very grave and self-possessed, and she enchanted them all with her skilled playing of the lute. Catherine has taught her a lot, for she herself is a good lutenist. And Catherine is in her element, laughing and beautiful, gently flirting with the Lowland nobles while always retaining a royal dignity. We performed several Spanish dances this evening, and then she partnered Harry in a dance. The pair of them move with a grace and neatness that makes them seem one thing. Little has been seen of Henry or Philip, who have been closeted together almost incessantly. They seem to have taken a great liking to each other – and of course they have one important thing in common. They both hate the idea of losing power to Ferdinand.

9th February 1506

Henry announced today that a treaty of close friendship with Philip has been signed. A whole string of royal marriages has been proposed as well. Mary is promised to Philip's young son, Charles, and Henry himself may possibly marry Philip's sister, Margaret of Savoy, though the lady has not been consulted about it. And Harry, it is suggested, could take as his bride Philip's daughter, Eleanor. I saw the shadow that crossed Catherine's face when she heard this. She is still utterly convinced that Harry is hers, but I cannot see how they can consider her a possibility now that her father has become the common enemy of Philip and Henry.

Harry was not present to hear these proposals. He has been sent at the head of a big retinue to fetch Juana from the West Country. Bets are being laid as to whether he will succeed, but I am sure he will. Nobody could refuse Harry when confronted by the full force of his charm and determination.

10th February 1506

He succeeded! Juana is here, white faced and huge-eyed, a little inclined towards tears – but surely not mad? She greeted King Henry with tremulous dignity, and as he gave her his arm to escort her in, I saw him look down at her with a curiously tender concern. Philip, on the other hand, greeted his wife with no more than conventional courtesy, and I saw her lips quiver as he walked away, though she managed to retain her composure.

Henry announced this evening that Philip has agreed to hand over the fugitive Earl of Suffolk, who has been living in the Netherlands for many years. The two royal men are on fire with their friendship and the power of the promises they have made to assist each other against all enemies, and Uncle Rod has sent a desperate message to Ferdinand of Aragon, warning him of the forces allied against him.

Tomorrow Catherine and her remaining retainers are to be sent back to Richmond, so she has had little chance to talk to her sister. And I have a new reason to regret leaving here. Tonight, I met a man who enchants me. He was sitting by the lily pool where great goldfish swim slowly under the round leaves. I had gone out to cool my flushed face, heated from dancing, and did not see him until he said, "It's better out here. Sane."

He came with Philip's entourage. He is their court jester, and they call him "Mr John" – perhaps that's as close as they can get to his real name, Michel Valjean. Or perhaps he took it as a stage name. I find myself remembering every word of the conversation I had with him. Such a down-to-earth conversation, about the absurdities of royalty and the dangers and pleasures of trying to cheer them up. "Your King Henry is hardly a laugh a minute, is he?" he said. "Hard work getting him to crack a smile. But he gave me ten pounds for amusing him, so I must have done something right."

He took my hand when we turned to come in, and ran his thumb over my knuckles. "A nice hand," he said. "Practical."

But tomorrow I have to go back to Richmond.

1st April 1506

All Fools' Day. So I think of my Fool, of course. My Michel. Foolishly, I expect. He has moved on now, to other courts, other fishponds, warm and still in the heat of Spain.

28th June 1506

Prince Harry's fifteenth birthday.

For us, there is no cause for celebration. Again, we shift in our ragged clothes from one contemptible place to another. When we came back to Richmond, we were put in rooms above the stable, dusty and mouse-infested, and now we are in a filthy, run-down manor in Fulham.

Nobody grumbles any more, we are past that. Everyone is aware of Catherine's simmering rage, but the determination in her set face commands respect. There are no carping remarks now about her pawning off the remaining plate and jewels, though we all know the goldsmiths charge her high interest rates, fearing they will never see their money again. Occasionally Henry gives her a hundred pounds or so, but it is swallowed up at once in reclaiming some of the pawned treasure. She cannot be stripped of everything, she says, if she is to have some self-respect when she marries Harry. I can't understand how she goes on believing this will happen.

18th October 1506

An extraordinary blow has fallen. We heard today that Philip of the Netherlands is dead. Philip the Handsome, as they all called him. Philip the Faithless, breaker of Juana's heart. Philip the friend of Henry and newly arrived king of Castile.

What will happen now? I suppose this means Ferdinand will resume his throne, ruling on behalf of Juana, whom he has always declared to be insane.

I am kept busy mending Catherine's gowns. I darn the tears and thin patches, then decorate them with flat-stitch embroidery, but nobody is taken in. We are destitute.

19th October 1506

I walked to the Strand late this afternoon, to see my uncle. He begins to look very old and worn. He says that now Philip is dead, Henry will have to win the favours of Emperor Maximilian, Philip's father. No lucky storm will blow him into Henry's court, so other means must be found. Henry is going to lend him 100,000 gold crowns.

23rd October 1506

A letter came from Mama today. She tells a terrible story about Juana. She would not leave Philip's body, sitting beside it in the chapel day and night, not seeming to hear what anyone said to her. When at last she fell asleep, they took it out of her sight, but she woke in a frenzy and summoned her servants, and when she found the coffin she bade her men take it on their shoulders and follow her, and she set out across the hills in a strange, wild procession with her dead husband. Heaven knows what has happened now – Mama does not say.

1st March 1507

Harry's elder sister, Margaret, gave birth to a son ten days ago. He is the first of a new generation of Tudors – that is, if they will think of him as a Tudor up there in Scotland. The boy is to be called James, after his father. I can hardly meet Catherine's eye, knowing what everyone is saying. If only she had managed to give Arthur a son, we would have had a royal boy here in London. As it is, this newborn half-Scot stands next to Harry and even, at some time in the future, above him, for this new James could inherit the crowns of both England and Scotland.

13th July 1507

Catherine is triumphant. After all these years, her father has sent her 2,000 ducats, apparently justifying all her faith in him. Now that Philip is dead, Ferdinand is again secure as the ruler of Spain, and he needs to patch up his damaged friendship with England. Perhaps I am cynical, but I suspect that his sudden generosity is more to please Henry than his daughter – but I will not say so, of course.

Catherine sat down at once to write a long letter of thanks to her father, and as she sealed it, she told me she had asked him to send a different ambassador. She made no explanation, just said we needed someone new. Did I not love her like a sister, I would feel deeply hurt.

2nd August 1507

I see now what Catherine was after. A fat package arrived from Spain this morning, and it contained the official papers which make Catherine herself Ferdinand's ambassador. Uncle Rod was at the court, and when he heard this he put his fingers to his forehead and closed his eyes in despair.

I, too, find it hard to believe Catherine can be a diplomat. She is clever, certainly, and tenacious, but her iron determination to marry young Prince Harry and be the Queen of England colours all her thinking, and I doubt whether she has it in her to learn the subtle arts of statesmanship. But I may be wrong. She learns fast.

3rd September 1507

Michel is here! A servant said this morning, with the curl of the lip I am used to, "There is a person in the kitchen wishing to see you."

And there he was, thinner than ever after long weeks of travel on foot. There was no place for him in the Spanish court once Philip had died, and he is going to make his way to the Netherlands, where Philip's eight-year-old son Charles is being cared for until such time as he is old enough to marry Mary.

If Michel secretly hoped he would be taken on as court jester here, he is out of luck, alas. Henry's generosity on the previous occasion was, I'm afraid, more to impress Philip with his careless munificence than to reward Michel's talent, and there are already a number of fools and entertainers here, some of them "innocents" whose drooling antics never make me smile.

Michel is not a welcome guest. He sleeps in the hay-loft and, did I not take him bread and meat scrounged from the kitchen, he would have nothing.

We walk together in the evenings and kiss, and I wish with all my heart that I could be with him always – but we can make no plans. Michel says he has no belief in plans, anyway. "Any wise man should lock them in a box and throw away the key," he says. "Half the world consists of key-seekers, you see, and what would they do if keys were not thrown away for them to seek?" I love him so much.

9th October 1507

The King is interested in marrying Juana. Catherine is all in favour of it. She has started to think diplomatically now and actually consults Uncle Rod quite often, with a new respect for his opinions. She can see that the alliance Henry hopes to forge with Philip's father, Maximilian (a brigand of a man, if you ask me), spells out a terrible danger to her father, so any link between England and Spain is to be welcomed.

Henry is concerned about the question of Juana's sanity, of course, having heard the tale of the mad coffin-carrying. My uncle assures him that Juana was simply driven beyond endurance by her beloved husband's flagrant infidelity to her. It is true that she did once attack one of his mistresses with a pair of scissors but, given steady kindness and care, she would very probably recover her stability. Henry was much taken with her during her short visit, and likes to regard her as an ill-used woman who is waiting for him to rescue her. The Tudors are incurably romantic.

24th December 1507

Henry's loan to Maximilian has had the desired effect. Last week the pair of them signed a treaty which pledges them to be allies, and in celebration we are all to have a merry Christmas, officially sanctioned. Free hogsheads of wine have been distributed throughout London, and singing and roistering is well under way. Bonfires burn in the streets and the church bells ring.

Needless to say, Catherine does not rejoice. She looks narrow-eyed and grim, but I cannot share her concerns at the moment. Today I had a letter from Michel, to read again and again, knowing his hand touched the paper and formed the words. I am as happy as any of the people in the streets, and wish I could join them in their singing and dancing.

14th January 1508

Catherine is demanding again that her father must send a new ambassador, but for a different reason this time. We must have a man of good standing, she says. Both she and my uncle (who has not been paid for many years) are too shabby and poor to be treated with any respect at court. It is time Spain was represented by a man of some grandeur.

16th February 1508

Ferdinand evidently saw the sense of Catherine's request. A new ambassador arrived today. His name is Gutierre Gomez de Fuensalida, and he is indeed grand – positively arrogant, in fact. He wears his fine clothes with the panache of a matador, and seems to regard Henry as the bull of England – a country which, he says, only understands a rough hand. Catherine enjoys his flamboyant company, but Uncle Rod is appalled. He is in bed with gout, but he sent his son Gonsalvo to warn Fuensalida to tread carefully, as relations between England and Spain are in a very delicate state.

Fuensalida took no notice but marched straight in to see the King, who has been ill with a chest complaint this winter. No wonder he felt so sure of himself – he had brought with him Catherine's long-unpaid dowry, 65,000 ducats of Aragon!

Suddenly, Catherine is back in favour. Fuensalida reported that Henry, though weak and forbidden to talk for long, spoke of her with great warmth and said there was nobody he would rather see as wife to his son.

"Didn't I tell you!" Catherine said to me this evening, sketching a dance across the floor in her delight. "Now we'll see!" But I feel uneasy about the new ambassador. Already people are finding him rude and objectionable, and I fear we are in for trouble.

19th February 1508

Trouble, indeed. It turns out that the 65,000 ducats does not represent the whole of Catherine's dowry. The rest is to be paid in jewellery and plate. Henry's officers asked whether the ambassador had brought these articles with him, and he pointed out that Catherine had been supplied with them in 1501, when she had married Arthur. But those had become Arthur's property when he had taken Catherine as his wife, the officers pointed out. Was Ferdinand now trying to pay his daughter's dowry with goods already in English possession? And why had he kept Catherine so deprived of her rightful dowry that she was forced to pawn these goods?

Fuensalida promptly pointed out that it was Henry's miserliness that had driven her to do this, and the meeting turned into a shouting match.

4th March 1508

Henry is recovered enough now to deal with Fuensalida himself, but every time they meet, it ends in a quarrel. My uncle, also a little better though still hobbling, does what he can to soothe the King's feelings and moderate Fuensalida's behaviour, so of course he is accused afresh of being on Henry's side. A dreadful situation.

27th March 1508

There is sad news from Scotland. Margaret has lost her baby son, little James. He died just a month ago, on February 27th, six days after his first birthday. She expects a second child this summer, but my heart goes out to her, especially as she stands in the middle of a worsening disagreement between England and Scotland. To have an English royal father and a Scottish royal husband puts her in a terrible position.

Last week Henry arrested the Earl of Arran for travelling across England without the necessary papers when he was on his way home to Edinburgh from France. The papers were just a technicality that Henry could have overlooked – but he knew the Earl had been conferring with Louis XII in Paris, and felt sure the French and the Scots were ganging up against England.

Unfortunately, the Earl is a cousin of King James, and a close personal friend, so there is great Scottish fury at his arrest. Catherine thinks Henry was perfectly justified. Although she likes Margaret, and is sorry for her, she has no patience with the Scots. As far as she can see, their old friendship with France makes them the enemies of Spain and of England. She reminds me so much of her dead mother these days. Queen Isabella, too, saw things in black and white. Those who were not with her were against her, with no word to be said in their favour. Thomas Wolsey has been sent to Edinburgh to try to smooth things over. I hope he succeeds.

21st June 1508

I cannot believe what has happened. Poor Uncle Rod – the whole thing is appalling. He was at a long, difficult meeting this afternoon with the King and the new ambassador, Fuensalida, about the situation between Scotland and France. Things are a little better since Wolsey's intervention, and Uncle Rod managed to persuade the King to be slightly more friendly to Catherine's father in Spain – but when they emerged from the chamber, Fuensalida turned on my uncle, shouting that his "pussyfoot tactics" were useless. Why did he not *demand* that Henry treat Ferdinand with more respect?

For once in his life, my uncle lost his temper. "I can do no more!" he shouted back. "I cannot twist the ears of the King of England!" And at that point, Fuensalida produced a letter from King Ferdinand and gave it to him. It was a letter dismissing Dr Rodrigo De Puebla from his post. He then said, with a triumphant smile on his face, that he had been carrying two letters from the Spanish king ever since his arrival here, one praising De Puebla for his excellent work, and the other dismissing him. Fuensalida had been waiting to choose which one to deploy. And he had now chosen.

I am so angry. This arrogant, tactless, trouble-making man has undone all Uncle Rod's years of faithful work, and he has proved, too, that Ferdinand never really trusted my uncle or liked him. I didn't know at first what had happened, but when I saw my uncle leaving the palace, he looked old and shrunken, and leaned heavily on the arm of his servant. I was so troubled that I ran up to ask if he was all right, and he shook his head. I went with him to his lodgings and stayed there for the night, sleeping on the couch in his room. He seems utterly collapsed.

22nd June 1508

Uncle Rod is still in his bed. He says he will never get up again. This morning he wrote a letter to King Ferdinand, then sealed it and gave it to me. "Make sure it is sent, my dear," he said. "There is no one else I can trust." Then he said it would be his last letter. "I will not have to trouble you again." I wept as I took it from his hand, but he seems beyond tears.

15th July 1508

The court has moved to Windsor where we are wretchedly quartered in rooms above the stables. I hate to be so far from Uncle Rod.

2nd August 1508

We have just heard that Margaret had a little girl two weeks ago, but the child did not live, and Margaret is ill. How ironic it is that King James has so many healthy children by his various mistresses, but his legal wife struggles to produce a living baby.

Henry has released the Earl of Arran from prison, and James has promised that he will not send an army to France, to fight on the side of the French king. Catherine gave a cynical smile when she heard this. "An easy promise," she said. "So he keeps his army in Scotland – but who is to say he will not attack us from across our northern border? He has made no promise about that."

20th September 1508

The whole court fled to the country three weeks ago, in panic because of an outbreak of plague in London. They took every available horse and carriage and all the supplies they needed, but not one of them suggested that Catherine should go with them. We were left here in Windsor, in our squalid rooms over the empty stables, and we foraged in the garden and the fields for food. It was humiliating that the peasants, who are so poor, gave us milk and cheese. Catherine assured me she would pay them, but I don't know how. Maybe she still has a few valuables that she can pawn, but if so, she keeps them hidden. However, we did not die or even become sick, and the courtiers are back now, chattering and gossiping like a flock of starlings.

They are all hysterically convinced that Henry means to attack Spain, and Fuensalida has actually written to Ferdinand, asking him to send a ship so that Catherine and her remaining household can be taken back to Granada before war breaks out.

Catherine is furious with him. He had no right to send such a letter without consulting her, she says. She has not struggled through all these years to cave in now, and whatever happens, she is staying here.

28th September 1508

I begged a lift to the Strand with a court lady who was going to visit her sister in London, and spent a day with Uncle Rod. He is still in bed, looking frail. I told him, truthfully, that Catherine now detests Fuensalida, and wishes she had listened more carefully to Uncle Rod's advice, and he smiled wearily. "History will judge," he said. He is hardly eating anything, and the skin is loose on his bony hands. I don't know what to do. I so much wish Michel was here. But at least Gonsalvo and his wife come often to see my uncle, so I know he is looked after.

1st October 1508

A letter from Mama came today. In Spain, too, people are afraid of an attack from Henry – though they are more afraid of the French. For the first time, Mama chides me for having fallen in love with a Frenchman. Couldn't I have found a nice Spaniard, she asks? But Michel has not been in France for years – he is a man of all nations. How I hate this wrangling and distrust.

Mama says Juana is now a prisoner, locked up by her father. Nobody knows if she is truly insane, but Ferdinand is ruling in her place, and he is making sure to keep her away from the public eye.

12th October 1508

Oh, what a rumpus! Catherine found out this morning that Fuensalida has been sending the plate, jewels and money that were meant to pay the last of her dowry out of the country "for safe keeping" in the Netherlands, because he is so sure there will be war between England and Spain. This all emerged when he walked into her room this morning and told her she must not go to the ceremony of Mary's betrothal.

Mary, Harry's little sister, is thirteen now, and when Philip and Juana came here because of the storm, she was promised to their son Charles. Catherine is very fond of Mary, and she was outraged by Fuensalida's high-handed order. It would be an unthinkable insult to Henry and the whole royal family to stay away from the ceremony. Catherine shouted at the ambassador, telling him he had no idea of manners or courtesy and was totally unfitted to be a diplomat. (In which I agree with her.) He tried to stand his ground, but she jumped to her feet and snatched up her embroidery scissors, and I think he really believed she might attack him. Anyway, he fled, and Catherine went rampaging to the King.

13th October 1508

When Fuensalida rode into Court this morning, the King's servants simply took his horse by the bridle and turned it round, directing the ambassador out again. Henry has refused to see him any more.

I sent a note to Uncle Rod, telling him of this in hopes it would cheer him up.

15th October 1508

The messenger who took my note brought no reply. He said my uncle seemed listless and ill. Catherine caught me weeping and asked what was the matter, and I told her. She promises she will send her own doctor to him. I hope it may do some good.

3rd November 1508

A short letter came from Uncle Rod today, written in his own hand, for which I thank God. I must not worry about him, he says. Gonsalvo or Bianca come every day, sometimes with their little son Miguel, and his landlady is kind. As to death, he says, that is not a thing to be feared. It is only a return to the mystery in which we existed before we were born. At the end he added a guarded sentence. "Gonsalvo will say for me that which should be said." He means *kaddish*, the Jewish prayer for the dead. Tears come to my eyes at that, but I am not sure why.

20th December 1508

Mary's betrothal has been celebrated with the usual splendour. Though still only thirteen, she was wonderfully composed, and a long account of the whole ceremony has been written in Latin, to be widely circulated. A translation in Spanish is to go to King Ferdinand.

As Michel might say, with a straight face, "I'm sure he'll love it."

And now we are to have another merry Christmas.

16th April 1509

King Henry is gravely ill. Here at Richmond, the palace which he designed and built, he fights for each laboured breath. The doctors are with him constantly, but I fear he is beyond the help of their leeches and potions. The court is hushed, and there is a constant murmur of prayer.

Nobody prays for my old uncle, who also lies waiting for his death, though in complete tranquillity. A message came from Gonsalvo yesterday, to say I should come if I wished to see him still alive, and Catherine said I must go at once. I don't know how she arranged it, but I was taken that morning by boat down the river to the Strand, with a manservant to look after me.

It seemed strange that the spirit still inhabited Uncle Rod's bony frame, so wasted and fleshless has he become, but he smiled when he saw me. I had to bend close to hear what he was trying to say. "There is nothing to do." It was just a whisper, then he closed his eyes in great tiredness. I still wonder what he meant. A life's work completed, perhaps, and the last ends tied up. Or maybe he was thinking of the wreckage that had been made of his skilled care, and the braggart non-diplomacy that had replaced it. Nothing to be done. The nations are heading for war.

17th April 1509

I wish I had not come back to Richmond last night. I should have sent the man back alone. I should have stayed. Uncle Rod died at dawn this morning, and I was not there. Gonsalvo sent a rider to Richmond with a letter to tell me what had happened. I cannot stop weeping.

21st April 1509

Henry VII of England is dead.

Such a public death. Not for him the obscurity of a small bedroom in a street near the river – Henry died with statesmen round his bed and the royal coat of arms above him. I felt bitter at first, but this evening I know I would not have wanted Uncle Rod to have been subjected to such a blaze of morbid interest. He died as he would have wished, with his son beside him and the murmured chant of an ancient prayer in his ears.

Henry, too, was watched over by his son in the slow days of his dying. Young Harry was with him constantly – but not just out of compassion. Together, the son and the dying father agreed on how the kingship should continue, and how England should stand among the other nations.

I knew nothing of this, of course, until Catherine, fresh from a meeting with Prince Harry, burst into the room where I was mending a dress yet again, and seized my hands, whirling me into a dance. "Eva! Do you know what the King's last words were? He said Harry and I must wed! We must marry before the coronation, so the people will have a new king and his queen. I have won, Eva! I've won, I've won!"

It's hard to believe, but it seems to be true. We can hardly celebrate when the King's body lies in state, awaiting burial, but all the Spaniards here are in a state of suppressed excitement. And Catherine herself seems to radiate pure joy.

11th May 1509

Yesterday was the King's funeral. Five black horses drew his carriage through black-shrouded streets. And Harry, or Henry, as I suppose I should now call him – Henry VIII of England – will marry Catherine in a month's time at the Church of the Observant Friars, by Greenwich Palace – the place where he was christened eighteen years ago.

Fuensalida is utterly confounded. He could not believe it when young Henry told him of his father's death-bed instruction. He walks about in silent consternation, like a man whose world has fallen about his ears, and he will have to retrieve all the money and valuables he spirited away to Flanders. "Everybody makes mistakes," Henry told him kindly when he gave this instruction. But the corners of his mouth twitched, and everyone saw his amusement. Henry is not to be trifled with, though. Catherine told me in a private moment this evening that he has already made arrangements for Fuensalida to be returned to Spain.

3rd June 1509

When will I get time to write a proper entry again? There is such a frenzy of cutting and stitching that I never have a free moment. Catherine's little household has to leap from obscurity to a queen's opulence, and we are so taken by surprise that we hardly know where to start. Lady Margaret Beaufort, who is regent of the country during this time between kings, has helped us by making her own stocks of silks and velvets available and by lending us sempstresses and embroidresses. Luckily the daylight is long at this time of the year, for some of the detailed work is hard to do by the glow of candles. We work at such a rate that it's a kind of madness, but as Michel said once, it's better to be mad than dull. Nobody could call it dull here now. Not any more.

24th June 1509 Midsummer Day

At last! Henry VIII of England and Catherine, Princess of Aragon and Wales (I feel I must give them their full titles) were crowned King and Queen of England today after their private marriage yesterday in Greenwich. They spent the night at the Tower of London, as tradition demands, and the waiting crowds yelled and cheered when they saw them. Henry looked magnificent, so tall and broad, every inch a king, clad in richly embroidered cloth of gold and his hair a red-gold colour too. Catherine rode in a white silk litter carried between two white palfreys, looking as young and untouched by the years as she was when she went to that other wedding. It seems now to have been so brief and so long ago that it might never have happened, except that these eight years of hardship and insult have been its direct result.

The people in the streets didn't care. For them, Catherine was their beautiful new bride-queen, and they roared their approval of her all the way to Westminster Abbey. We, her ladies, rode beside her on white horses, and our robes of blue velvet, edged with crimson, set off her silken whiteness perfectly. The streets were hung with scarlet cloth, thousands of yards of it, and the entire court was dressed in scarlet robes, richly furred. For weeks, Lady Margaret has been buying up all the cloth she could lay her hands on. What an amazing woman she is! At 66 years old, she has run the country since her son's death, and now she presides over the wedding and coronation of her grandson as well, with absolute efficiency. No wonder she looks exhausted.

When the procession had entered the Abbey, no one could hold the crowds back. They fell upon the white damask cloth that had lined the way in and hacked it to pieces, grabbing and snatching at scraps of it to take home in an almost religious frenzy, as though the tattered bits of silk they clutched were an actual part of royalty. But their avidness made me think of crows tearing at a dead lamb, and I found them frightening. Perhaps they frighten kings as well, which is why they like to show their wealth and power. And why any real trouble-maker is promptly hanged.

27th June 1509

The feasting goes on and on, in joyous celebration – and there is a sense of relief, too, as though we have all escaped from a crabbed hand that kept us from happiness. There is a new gaiety about the jousting and carnival, a new sense of youth and high spirits. Energy seems to radiate from Henry, who is free at last from that stuffy room with no door except the one into his father's chamber. He is laughing and tireless, charging across the tiltyard on the great stallion he rides, banqueting and dancing – but all the time his eyes seek Catherine's in an intimacy that almost makes me blush, and he constantly returns to her side to run his hand down her back and touch his lips to hers. She is his first love, and he cannot get enough of her.

Catherine matches him perfectly. She shares his joy in music and dancing, revels as he does in new clothes and the glory of jewels and rich embroideries, and yesterday she was out with him on a hunting expedition, strong and graceful on her white horse, a hawk on her wrist, truly the warrior queen's daughter. But she has learned much in these hard years, and she has a composure about her which compels her young husband's admiration. She is no longer a girl; she has become a graceful, wise young woman. She has had eight years to think about becoming Henry's queen, and now that it has come about, she is performing her new role faultlessly.

29th June 1509

Alas, Lady Margaret Beaufort died this afternoon, quite suddenly. She retired to her room after supervising yet another sumptuous meal of roast swan and fine wines, and fell into eternal sleep. Her death grieves me more than any I have known save that of Uncle Rod. Henry wept in Catherine's arms when he was told the news, though he quickly gathered his dignity as he had to. He is the king, even though he throws himself into his games of hunting and music and mock-war with a boy's intensity.

At least Lady Margaret lived to see the despatch brought by an envoy from Scotland this morning. A treaty of peace has been signed between England and Scotland, thank God, and the letter from King James that came with it was full of warm congratulations on Henry's marriage and coronation. Dare I hope these brothers-in-law will at last learn to trust each other?

Doubts nag at my mind. Henry announced the treaty as a triumph, and I am sure he is relieved to know that Scotland will not attack from the north should he go to war with France, but somehow I can see Uncle Rod shaking his head.

3rd July 1509

As one might expect, Lady Margaret left a careful, detailed will. Her library of glorious books is to go to the college she founded in Cambridge, though Henry has been given some of the best of them. He is the head of the family now, so he inherits the bulk of her estate, but she shared her jewellery between the royal grand-daughters and Catherine. A secret came to light, too. When Arthur died, his possessions were shared among the family, but because Margaret was due to marry James and go to Scotland, her bequest of gold and jewels and plate was kept in trust for her, and she has never yet received it.

Henry's expression did not change when this was read out, but I thought it was rather disgraceful. Uncle Rod left me some books, which I treasure, but how would I have felt if Gonsalvo had refused to give them to me? Such a thing never crossed my mind, of course – or his. He had the books carefully packed and sent to me only a week later. But the property of royal families is different. It represents bargaining power, and I suppose the old King could not bear the idea of such valuable stuff going to Scotland, a country that was always a potential enemy. As so often, I feel sorry for Margaret – but at least she is genuinely happy in her marriage. Catherine says her letters always speak with pride and affection of her Scottish husband, whom she obviously adores. Perhaps my pity is misplaced, and I should envy her.

22nd July 1509

Michel is here! No creeping through the back door this time – he has come as the court jester with a delegation from Prince Charles, Philip's son, the boy who will marry Mary.

I have hardly managed to see him. There was the inevitable banquet tonight, and Michel was joking and clowning. Henry laughed so much that he spluttered wine all over his gold-embroidered doublet – messy man – but he gave Michel six pounds at the end of the evening, and summoned him to his private chambers, that he and the Queen might have some further amusement. Sometimes I curse Henry's inexhaustible energy.

23rd July 1509

Dear Lord, I give thanks for this day! Early this morning, I heard a tune being whistled in the garden, and jumped up to look out. There was Michel, standing on the grass all silver with dew, smiling up at me. He held out his hands, and I said, "Wait." I ran down just as I was, in my nightdress, with my feet bare and my hair loose. And he dropped to one knee, laughing and yet serious, and . . . asked me to be his wife.

When I could catch her alone I told Catherine, and she kissed me and wished me well. There was a time when we would have hugged each other, but she is the queen now, and even I, her childhood friend, have to remember that. But she still loves me, and promised she would tell Henry and ask him to do what he could for us. She kept her word, for he summoned Michel and me to go and see him in his private chamber. We did not know what to expect, but he seemed amused and gave us his blessing. Then he said the Queen did not want to lose me, and for a moment my heart lurched in panic, lest I should be forced to stay in London when Michel goes back to the Netherlands. But Henry smiled, looking very pleased with himself. He had arranged an exchange of fools, he said. Michel would stay here and in his place John Scot would go back to young Charles. John Scot is a dwarf who came here with the party that returned from escorting Margaret to her wedding in Edinburgh, and I have never much liked him. Perhaps Henry feels likewise, because he grinned and said he had the best of the bargain.

Michel turned at the door to doff his cap with a courtly bow, and managed to get the feather stuck between his knees. I tugged at his arm, fearing he had gone too far, but Henry roared with laughter. Michel says clowning is always about going too far. That's why it's funny, he says. You live on the edge of disaster, but just avoid it.

Don Alessandro will marry us in September. I am so happy that I can hardly breathe.

21st September 1509

I have hardly thought about writing my diary. With Michel here, I am not lonely, so I haven't felt the same need to use the blank pages as a substitute for someone to talk to. And on the best day of my life I was too busy living it to think of writing about it. We were married here in the chapel at Windsor, and Catherine came, together with dozens of courtiers both English and Spanish. There was a feast afterwards, followed by music and dancing, and for us there was no embarrassing ritual of bishops and blessings. Our first night as a married couple was private to us.

Catherine gave me a delicate gold pendant set with a diamond and small sapphires and, as a better present still, whispered her secret in my ear. She is with child! I hug the knowledge as an added delight in that glorious day, even though everyone knows it now.

I pray that Catherine's baby will live and be healthy. Michel says the newborn sons and daughters of queens take one look at the world, realize they are royal and promptly die. Who can blame them, he says? I should not laugh, but I do. My life is full of laughter now.

14th November 1509

News has just reached us from Scotland that Margaret has given birth to a son. The child seems healthy, and he is to be called Arthur, in memory of Margaret's brother. Perhaps Margaret has been thinking of the bequest Arthur left her, and hopes this gentle hint may nudge Henry towards sending it. "She'll be lucky," Michel says. And he's probably right.

30th January 1510

Catherine has given birth before her due time, to a little girl who was dead when she came into the world. All over the court, I hear people say, "At least it was a girl", trying to console themselves. The loss of a son would have been so much worse. I went to see Catherine this evening. She is not seriously ill, thank God, but she is white-faced and wretched, and I could not find words to comfort her. We both know childbirth is a dangerous business – but at least she herself is alive. So many women die.

I could not bring myself to tell her that I am myself pregnant. To tell the truth, it frightens me a little, but Michel reminds me of what he said about royal children. Our baby will not be burdened with the hopes of nations, so it will be carefree and healthy.

It may not be merely the hopes of nations that cast such a blight on the Tudor women's attempts to produce heirs. I have heard that an illness runs through the royal line, transmitted to their wives and affecting their unborn children, causing them to die in the womb or be born sickly and short-lived. Nobody says this aloud, but the rumour runs underground like the roots of sorrel, popping up in a new growth of gossip and head-shaking every time a royal child fails to live. I must not listen, in case my own baby is affected by the very idea. In any case, I'll be too busy for idle talk. I have to make little clothes and caps and shawls as well as keep up with my work at court. Catherine has entrusted me with the supervision of all the embroidery done by her staff of needlewomen, and while I am flattered, and pleased to have the money it brings, the next months are going to be frantically busy.

16th August 1510

Three days ago my daughter was born. She is pink and beautiful, and her name is Rosanna, Rose for her pinkness and health, and Anna because it is my mother's name. I have sent a letter to Mama with the news. How I wish she could be here!

Michel is so proud of his daughter. He cradles her lovingly, offering his finger to the grip of her little hand. Her birth was a long, agonizing struggle, but all that is easily forgotten in the joy of her living presence. Daily I thank God for her.

17th August 1510

As if to underline my good fortune, a messenger from Scotland today brought the news that Margaret's little son, Arthur, has died. This is the third child she has lost. Michel remarked that Henry will be pleased. "That leaves the field open for him and Catherine," he said. A cynical observation, but perhaps it is true. Catherine is pregnant again, and the whole court is praying for her.

12th October 1510

We have a new ambassador, a replacement for Fuensalida. This one, too, is a strutting popinjay, but it doesn't matter much. Henry turns to Catherine whenever he needs guidance, and she is always ready with a quiet word of advice or the supply of a needed fact.

She amazes me now. I'd never have thought she could play so many parts, all of them with such grace and self-assurance. Henry is still a boy at heart – perhaps some boyhood is owed to him after the years of being confined by his careful father – and he loves to play games. Sometimes he and his friends dress up as Robin Hood and his outlaws, or as Moors with black faces, or booted Russians, and come bursting into the room where Catherine and her ladies are sitting, as if to take us prisoner. Catherine always jumps up and shrieks with just the right mixture of delight and theatrical terror, joining in his game because she loves him and because he is her king.

At other times she is very much the diplomat. Henry has been worrying about Ferdinand having taken a French wife and (worse) having signed a peace pact with France, but Catherine looked at him calmly with her grey eyes. "My lord," she said respectfully, "you are a great statesman; you will understand my father's motives. In his place, threatened by attack from France, would you not play for time? Make a marriage, sign a pact, buy a few months of safety? If you wish it, he will be on your side when the time comes. Believe me." And he had no choice but to smile down at her – she comes barely to his shoulder – then take her in his arms and call her his clever little vixen.

Even Catherine can't always restrain Henry, though. He's like a young bull let out of his shed in the spring, Michel says, ready to charge at anything that catches his eye. He loves the idea of war. To him it means honour and glory, a chance to be thought of with the same respect as that earlier Henry, Henry V, who beat the French at Agincourt. He is so full of this idea that such things as tact and carefulness are often forgotten. At a meeting with the French ambassador last week, he quite forgot that Catherine had advised him to follow her father's example and sign a temporary peace treaty. When this was suggested, he blew up instantly and roared, "*I* ask for peace with France? Who dares say so?" The tale has run round the court with much delighted gossip about how Catherine had to call for an adjournment and some wine while she calmed her husband down and made him see sense.

She has succeeded in bringing Henry and her father together, at least for the purpose of this proposed war. Ferdinand has reminded Henry that the area surrounding the French city of Bordeaux used to be under English rule until about 60 years ago. Its citizens, he says, are longing to have Henry as their king. Michel snorted with laughter when he heard this, and said the French would rather be ruled by a pig than by Henry. (That, of course, is strictly between ourselves.) Meanwhile, Catherine expects her next baby in January, and Henry is pleased with himself. God willing, he will become a father and the liberator of the suffering people of France. Or so he hopes.

1st January 1511

There could not be a better start to this new year. Catherine has given birth to a boy, and all the church bells are ringing. The court has gone into instant rejoicing, and Henry is cock-a-hoop with pride. The child will be called after him, of course, another Henry to come to the throne in his turn, and all London knows a royal prince has been born. Bonfires burn in the streets and cannon are booming from the Tower.

Nobody seems to take much notice of Catherine in all this, but I am so happy for her, knowing as I do the delight of a living baby. Sometimes Michel picks Rosanna up by her little feet and holds her upside down in the air. I was horrified the first time he did it, but he says she may as well get used to the idea that the world is topsy turvy. And she seems to love it, crowing and gurgling with delight. I am making a new cap for her, sewn with tiny blue beads and satin ribbon.

21st February 1511

The celebrations were short-lived, as was the little prince. He died early this morning after barely seven weeks of quiet, sickly life. Catherine is distraught, and Henry walks about with an ashen face. This is the greatest blow he has ever suffered, and he has no way to combat it.

4th June 1511

Busy, busy, busy. Constant embroidery work for the court, and supervising all the other needlewomen as well. Michel says I am doing too much – looking after him and Rosanna is enough. Perhaps he is right. For a while, I thought I was pregnant again, but it came to nothing. I grieve a little for a child that might have been, even if it existed only in my imagination.

Henry's preparations for war continue. They seem to be some consolation to him for his lost son, but Catherine looks older, and has lost much of her happiness.

12th March 1512

I still have little time to write – or inclination, in fact. The days go by so fast, and Rosanna is walking now. Not just walking, but climbing and scrambling and getting into everything. She babbles in a mixture of English and Spanish, for I have always spoken to her in my own language, and she even knows a few French words as well, from Michel.

This delights him, but it would be rash to speak French outside the safety of our own quarters. War fever is mounting, and the Pope has called on all the rulers of Europe to join in what he calls the Holy League against France. The Pope hates Louis because he was rash enough to criticize the Pope for having fathered so many illegitimate children. I cannot help feeling that these war games are a personal sport between men of power. Henry has bought 48 immense guns, each one over seven feet long, and has given them names and badges, as if they were living things.

17th March 1512

King James of Scotland has written to all the kings of Europe, calling for peace. We are all Christians, he says, and should learn to tolerate each other. I think he is right, but Catherine is contemptuous. She says James has no right to call himself a peacekeeper. "Look how often he has raided England's northern border," she says.

Michel has a great respect for James. Court jesters know more than most people about what goes on in high circles, and they gossip among themselves constantly, of course, passing on any bits of scandalous news and scraps of inside information. Knowing what is happening is all part of their job. Those of them who know James all like him. He's a thoughtful man, they say, practical and yet imaginative, and he adores his wife even though he was so wild as a young man. Margaret expects another baby very soon. Michel says he sometimes wishes we were at the Scottish court instead of this one, but yesterday he added that it couldn't be as ridiculous as the English one. "This lot fancy themselves so important that they're half off their heads," he said. "Fascinated with themselves. Quite absurd. And what would a jester do without absurdity? I'd be no good with James – he's much too sensible."

Henry would be outraged. He likes to think of himself as extremely sensible. He spends a lot of time with Wolsey now, and is beginning to value his opinion more than Catherine's. Wolsey is what Michel calls "one of the New Men". His father was a butcher in Ipswich, and he climbed out of the blood and sawdust through sheer cleverness. Henry is a New Man, too, I suppose, unlike James, who comes of the ancient Stuart line. He looks ahead to a grand future, and picks his friends accordingly. Wolsey is the only cleric I know who wears robes made from pure, heavy silk.

28th April 1512

Margaret's baby was born on the 10th of this month, and it is a boy, healthy and strong, the letter says. He, like his short-lived elder brother, will be called James. Perhaps Catherine and Henry, still childless, regret having sent her the Girdle of Our Lady, a most precious relic, reputed to work wonders for queens desiring the safe delivery of a child.

7th June 1512

Twelve thousand men have sailed for the Basque frontier between Spain and France, following 6,000 last week. Such numbers! They are under the command of the Marquess of Dorset, who seems to me a foppish gentleman for the business of war, but perhaps he will surprise us. And now we wait for news.

10th July 1512

Dorset's army waits at San Sebastian to be joined by the Spanish troops of Ferdinand. It must be terribly hot in that place between the mountains and the Bay of Biscay, and the English will not understand that one has to have a siesta in the afternoon. It's very unhealthy to be out in the blaze of midday. The French watch them and seem perplexed, the despatch says. No shot has yet been fired.

Catherine is frowning and puzzled. Her father should have met Dorset long before now, with cavalry troops and artillery as arranged. The English could not ship large numbers of horses, and they depend on Ferdinand to supply them with mounts. Something has gone wrong.

23rd July 1512

The court has begun to mutter that Ferdinand has betrayed Henry. Instead of meeting the English troops as he promised, he has gone straight to Navarre, where he is besieging that small kingdom, knowing the French will not come to its aid as they are still watching Dorset's army and waiting for it to make a move. But the English cannot move, for they still have no horses. They are sweltering in San Sebastian, bored and angry and drinking too much wine.

It's an embarrassing situation for Catherine. Her father it seems has deceived her as well as everyone else about his true intentions. Quite obviously, he has used the English troops to tie up the French while he, Ferdinand, gets on with taking Navarre. Catherine falls back on blaming the ambassador, Caroz, but he is as baffled as anyone else. And Henry, of course, is raging.

2nd September 1512

Another letter came from Dorset's army today, and its contents were soon common gossip. The men are on the point of mutiny. They are nearly all ill now, with a stomach sickness that has killed many of them. They blame the garlic! So stupid – but I can't help feeling sorry for them. Henry has sent a herald with a return message, telling Dorset the army must stay where it is for the winter, ready for a fresh campaign in the spring. "You see what I mean?" Michel said. "Totally absurd. They'll all be dead."

29th September 1512

Henry's herald was shouted down. The soldiers would not listen, and their yells turned into a chant of "Home! Home! Home!" Henry will have to give in.

11th December 1512

The wretched stragglers who were once an army have come home. And Ferdinand has sent an incredibly insulting message, saying the English troops were of such poor quality that he couldn't use them. He adds that he has had to make peace with the French for six months, for fear they might invade England, having seen how hopeless the English soldiers are.

Henry is gibbering with rage. He was all for hanging the Marquess of Dorset the moment he set foot in England, but Catherine managed to dissuade him. It would do his reputation no good, she said. Better by far to show the watching world that England is still a nation to be feared. He must prepare for war next year. And this time, he must win.

20th December 1512

James of Scotland is still trying to negotiate a peace between France and her enemies. He sent an envoy to Paris – or at least, he tried to, but Henry turned the man back at the border. It's hardly surprising, Michel says. Henry knows a French ship arrived at the Leith docks two weeks ago laden with wine and cloth of gold, but also with artillery guns of a new and very accurate kind, together with 300 cannon balls and a large quantity of gunpowder.

13th January 1513

Henry was in a fresh storm of rage this morning. His spies in Scotland tell him that James has received a letter from the French queen, Anne of Brittany, with which she sends her glove and a turquoise ring, begging him to come to the aid of France when England and Spain attack her.

"She sent him her *glove*," Michel said, exhausted after the hard work of restoring the King to something like good humour. "You know what that means. It is the traditional sign given to a knight by a lady in distress. Chivalry will not allow him to ignore it."

Henry is infuriated that his brother-in-law takes up this high moral tone – "Posing," he bellowed, "as the saintly peace-keeper of Europe!" Henry hates peace. Enemies are a necessary and enjoyable evil, part of the great game of war, but peace is the ultimate wet-blanket, undoing the game itself. We all breathed more easily when he went storming out to the river, there to be ferried down to Woolwich, to inspect the progress of his new ships that are being built. Whole forests have been cut down for the sake of this armada, and the sky seems strangely open and empty where the great oaks used to stand. But Henry loves his ships, specially the huge flagship, the *Great Harry*. Suits of armour arrive daily from Italy and Spain, together with hundreds of fine new swords and daggers, and he has twelve immense cannon, sent by Maximilian, which he calls *The Twelve Apostles*.

Both Catherine and Mary have received letters from Margaret in Scotland. She had a miscarriage in the autumn, and was ill for some time, and in recent weeks she has been much troubled by nightmares. She dreams constantly of her husband's death, and of standing alone on a high cliff in a desolate place, with the sea crashing on rocks a long way below her. She always sends loving wishes to Henry in her letters, but I doubt whether he writes back to her. Scotland, too, is part of the great game of war, and to see it through the eyes of his sister would be dangerously close to wishing for peace.

4th May 1513

Henry is deeply perturbed about the Queen of France's appeal to James. He has sent an envoy to Scotland – Nicholas West, the dry, virtuous Dean of Windsor – hoping to get a promise from James that he will not aid France in the coming war.

12th May 1513

West has returned, ruffled and angry, and the court is full of excited gossip, as usual. They try to pump Michel, who is closer to the King than any of them, but he tells them he is just the pet monkey, and hops and gibbers until they shrug and turn away. I know, as they do not, how much Henry confides in him, and what a strain it is to be called upon to find crumbs of comfort and amusement in a morass of bad news. West utterly failed to bribe James to stay on the English side. He failed, too, in a clumsy attempt to bribe Margaret, offering her the gold and jewels bequeathed to her by Arthur in return for a promise that she would persuade James not to help France. Margaret simply laughed and walked out, for which I admire her, and after that she removed herself and her small son, James, to the castle of Linlithgow. She is pregnant again, expecting a baby in the autumn, and I would hate to be in her situation, caught between two sides in the war which will now undoubtedly come soon.

30th June 1513

It has started. Henry and his great fleet have set sail, complete with all their guns and armour, banners, lances, provisions and horses (for he is taking his own cavalry this time). My fingers are sore from stitching, since this war is also a travelling pageant of Tudor glory. Every tunic and jerkin and cloak, every saddle-cloth and even every tent has been gold-embroidered, and the army set off under a moving forest of plumes and banners. We have used bale upon bale of cloth of gold, both red and white, and tissue of silver, as well as silks and velvets in crimson and blue and purple, and countless yards of green and white cloth have gone into the making of tents and covers for waggons. The armourers and smiths have been working equally hard, engraving designs of antelopes and swans on to breastplates and forging silver medallions for harnesses and little gold bells to tinkle on bridles. This is the greatest tournament of Henry's life, and he has revelled in every moment of it.

Catherine, too, has thrown herself into it all. She rode to Dover with Henry at the head of the long procession, and at the sea's edge he proclaimed her Governor of the Realm in his absence, and put her in charge of northern defences. I did not go, for I am certainly pregnant again now, and it is making me often sick. Catherine agreed that I could stay at home when Michel spoke to her on my behalf. I felt ashamed to do so, for Catherine herself is expecting a child, and I suspect that she must despise me for giving in to such weakness. She ignores her condition, just as her mother did, the battling Isabella. Those who came back say she made a fiery speech to the assembled men. I can imagine how her Spanish-accented English rang out over the breaking of the waves.

And now they are gone. Henry insisted on taking Michel with him, and Rosanna does not understand where Papa has gone. God keep him safe.

29th July 1513

A messenger brought news today that Henry met as arranged with the Emperor Maximilian's army, under the walls of a French town called Thérouanne. It was pouring with rain. Such a shame, when the army had set out looking so glorious in its red and gold and Tudor-green. And Maximilian's men were all in black. It must have amused Michel – Henry's troops decked out in magnificence while the old Habsburg bandit sticks to practicalities. He does not play at war; it is his business.

In Henry's absence, Catherine has at once set about the business of running the country. I realize now what a soldier she is by instinct, for the first thing she did was to send a large army northwards, to cover the Scottish border against attack. She intends to raise a second army of new recruits, to reinforce the first, which is under the command of the Earl of Surrey. "If James attacks, he will get his fingers burned," she said to me this evening. "And serve him right."

2nd September 1513

I pray for Michel's safety. Perhaps he is not in too much danger, for Henry's war seems to be little more than a glorified tournament. A few villages have been sacked and burned, but King Louis is mainly concerned with holding his advances in Italy, and has told his commanders merely to watch the English rather than engage with them. (Catherine receives daily despatches from Henry.) There has only been one skirmish so far, which ended in a spirited English chase after fleeing French cavalry. It sounds as if the whole campaign is, by Henry's standards, thoroughly enjoyable. All of us here are far more concerned with Scotland.

Margaret's last letter to her sister Mary spoke of continuing nightmares. She dreamed of the high cliff again, but, horrifyingly, she saw James fall to his death – and the diamonds in her jewel box had all turned to pearls, the emblems of widowhood. I never knew this was the meaning of pearls. We sewed so many of them into Catherine's veil for her first wedding to Arthur – and she was indeed a widow within a few months.

4th September 1513

Catherine's instincts were right. James has declared war on England. Everyone here is appalled, but Catherine is filled with energy and excitement. Her new troops are arriving by the hour, some of them from as far away as Wales and Cornwall, and she plans to ride with them herself for at least part of the way. I tried to tell her she should not do this. She carries a royal child within her, and strenuous days on the road could have a disastrous result. Both of us know that Isabella had several miscarriages because of taking part in warlike expeditions – but perhaps Catherine feels she can do no less. Michel would shake his head wearily. *Madness, madness.* I miss him so much.

8th September 1513

Catherine has set off for Buckingham at the head of her army. Wolsey's spies in the north reported that a group of wild Highlanders from the north of Scotland have already launched an attack, not waiting for King James, but they were quickly repulsed. James has gone to Linlithgow to say goodbye to Margaret.

12th September 1513

I can hardly bring myself to write about what has happened. I am shaken and sick at the thought of it, and glad in a way that this is almost the last page of my diary. I shall never keep another. Were it not for a kind of loyalty to Catherine, I would like to leave this court and live with Michel and our children as ordinary people do, knowing nothing of the great games of kings.

The Scottish army is utterly destroyed, and James is dead. Surrey met them in the Cheviot hills, at a place called Flodden. The Scots were tired from long marching, Wolsey's rider reports, and they had run short of food and ale. James made the mistake of ordering them to move the guns further up the ridge to a better position, but Surrey had plenty of time to deploy his troops, almost surrounding the Scots.

In three hours of fighting, 10,000 Scottish soldiers were killed. Ten *thousand*. There can hardly be an able-bodied man left in the country. The officers and nobility, too, were mown down, and at last James himself fell.

Catherine is still on her way to Buckingham, but her army will not be needed. This war, at least, is finished.

23rd September 1513

Catherine's expedition cost her dearly. On the night after her return, she lost the baby she had been expecting. Poor little future child – such an innocent casualty of war, and so deliberately put at risk, it seems to me. Catherine herself looks white-faced and exhausted, but she gave herself no rest after the miscarriage, and it has not stopped her from the grim business in which she is still taking part.

When she heard of James's death she ordered his body to be brought to London. I was with her when the captain of the travel-weary men came to report that this had been done. She went out with him, and bade me follow. I could not look at the wrapped and already stinking burden they carried, but she seemed exultant. The body must be taken to Henry in France, she said, that he might see for himself that the Scots had been vanquished.

An uneasy glance ran between the men, and their captain begged Catherine to excuse them from such a task. She looked at him with contempt, and turned on her heel.

Upstairs, she unwrapped the bundle of soiled clothing which the captain had given her, and held up a surcoat, gold-embroidered with the lion of Scotland. It was soaked with blood and slashed almost to ribbons. The captain had explained apologetically that after the battle the English troops had plundered the dead men who lay everywhere, stripping them of clothes and valuables. The body of the Scottish king, too, had been stripped, but the captain had managed to retrieve his coat. And as I watched her, sickened, Catherine smiled. "If I cannot send his dead enemy's body, Harry shall at least have his coat," she said. And in the afternoon of that same day, she despatched it to France.

28th September 1513

Michel is home, thank God, laughing about what he calls "Harry's summer circus". The real war was Catherine's, and it is Flodden that makes Europe's kings look with new respect at English fighting power.

Catherine spoke to me today of Margaret, whose child will be born with no father. Her little son, only eighteen months old, has been crowned James V of Scotland, but Margaret herself will rule as best she can over a country made derelict by the loss of its men. "I have sent people to comfort her," Catherine said. All her exultation had gone, and she looked drained of energy, her grey eyes shadowed with tiredness and distress. "Between us, Margaret and I must agree to keep the peace," she went on. "I am disbanding my army."

Her voice quavered a little, and she suddenly turned to me and wept. We were both aware that James, her brother-in-law, lies in the chapel here at Richmond, washed and embalmed and decently shrouded. The mute dignity of his dead presence makes it pitifully clear what Margaret has lost and what thousands of women have lost – 1,500 of them in England as well as the countless multitude in Scotland.

Catherine and I stood close, with our arms about each other as we have not done in many years. I knew she must be aware of the thickness of my body that is the coming baby, and ached with pity for her though I could say nothing about her own loss. After a few minutes she parted herself from me gently and wiped her eyes, then managed to smile. "Dear Eva," she said. "I hope the future will be kind to you."

With all my heart, I wish the same for Catherine. Proud, reckless, careful Catherine, my friend, my queen. May God guard her in what is to come.

Historical note

Catherine of Aragon and Henry were married just before Henry was crowned King of England in 1509. Their marriage lasted for nearly 20 years, and it seems that it was a happy one, at least at the beginning, even though the reasons for it were political and not romantic. After he married Catherine, Henry is reported to have said, "If I were still free, I would still choose her for wife above all others."

The marriage of Henry's sister Margaret to the Scottish king James IV had also taken place for political reasons: Scotland had a history of alliance with England's greatest enemy, France, and the marriage came a year after a peace treaty between Scotland and England. But not long after Henry VIII came to the throne, James tried to break the peace with England, despite being married to Henry's sister. While Henry was away in France, Catherine was left in charge of the country and it was under her rule that the English army beat the Scots at the Battle of Flodden. The victorious Catherine really did send the blood-stained coat of the dead James IV to Henry, as Eva reports in her diary. Later, in 1542, Henry's English army was to defeat the army of Henry's own nephew – Margaret's son, James V of Scotland. In 1514, Henry's younger sister Mary was married to Louis XII of France, another political royal marriage.

Catherine gave birth to five children, but only one of them survived for more than a few weeks – a girl, Mary, not the hoped-for boy who could continue the Tudor line. By the time Catherine was in her thirties she was no longer able to have children and Henry wanted an end to the marriage. In 1527 he began to try and arrange a divorce, which proved extremely difficult and took six years to achieve. Before Henry could marry Catherine, back in 1509, he had needed special permission from the Pope, as head of the Catholic Church, because Catherine was his brother's widow. Now, Henry argued that the marriage should never have taken place and could be "annulled" – declared invalid. The Pope wouldn't give his permission – it would have meant going against the previous Pope's authority (who had allowed Catherine and Henry to marry in the first place), and secondly he needed to keep the peace with the powerful Emperor Charles V, who was Catherine of Aragon's nephew and who held most of Europe. Finally, Henry made himself head of the Church in England, and got his divorce without permission from the Pope. These must have been sad and humiliating years for Catherine: Henry went so far as to imprison their daughter, Mary, when she protested against the divorce. Henry's actions not only affected Catherine but the whole country – breaking away from the Pope's authority meant that Henry would go on to reform the Church in England, taking away land, wealth and power from the monasteries, and England would eventually become a Protestant country.

Catherine had been a popular queen with the people of England, but Henry's next wife, Anne Boleyn, was not. He married Anne in 1533 and she had a child the same year – another daughter, Elizabeth, which did not please Henry, who refused to go to the christening.

Catherine died in 1536 – there were rumours that she was poisoned, some said by Anne Boleyn, but there's no evidence to suggest that this was true. Henry showed no grief at her death.

Famously, Henry was married to six different wives, but none of them – apart from Catherine of Aragon – lasted for more than a few years. Anne Boleyn was executed in 1536, accused of treason. Henry married Jane Seymour in the same year, who did provide him with the son he longed for but died soon after giving birth. His next three marriages, to Anne of Cleves, Catherine Howard and Catherine Parr, didn't produce any more children.

After his death in 1547, Henry's only son, Edward, became king at the age of nine, but died six years later. This meant that Mary, Catherine of Aragon's daughter with Henry, became queen. During her short reign she became known as Bloody Mary: she was fiercely Catholic, unlike her Protestant younger brother, and executed hundreds of Protestant "heretics". She died of influenza in 1558, leaving the throne to her half-sister Elizabeth (a Protestant), who would reign for 45 years before dying childless, the last of the Tudors.

Timeline of Tudor England

1485 Henry Tudor defeats Richard III at the Battle of Bosworth, and becomes Henry VII, the first Tudor king of England.

1486 Prince Arthur is born.

1491 Prince Henry (later Henry VIII) is born.

1501 Arthur marries Catherine of Aragon.

1502 Arthur dies.

1509 Henry VII dies. Prince Henry marries Catherine of Aragon and is crowned King Henry VIII.

1513 War with France and Scotland. James IV of Scotland dies at the Battle of Flodden Field.

1516 Catherine of Aragon has a daughter, Mary (later Queen Mary I).

1527 Henry starts his divorce from Catherine of Aragon.

1533 Henry marries Anne Boleyn. They have a daughter, Elizabeth (later Queen Elizabeth I).

1536 Anne Boleyn is beheaded. Henry marries Jane Seymour. Catherine of Aragon dies.

1536–9 The Reformation of the Church in England.

1537 Jane Seymour has a son, Edward (later Edward VI). She dies after the birth.

1540 Henry marries Anne of Cleves but they are divorced the same year. Henry marries Catherine Howard.

1542 Catherine Howard is beheaded.

1543 Henry marries Catherine Parr.

1547 Henry VIII dies. His only son becomes Edward VI of England.

1553 Edward VI dies. Catherine of Aragon's daughter, Mary, becomes Queen.

1554 Mary marries Philip of Spain.

1558 Mary dies. Elizabeth I becomes Queen of England.

1603 Elizabeth I, the last of the Tudor monarchs, dies.

Picture acknowledgments

P 131 (top)	Portrait of a woman, possibly Catherine of Aragon (1503/4), Michiel Sittow (1469-1525), Kunsthistorisches Museum, Vienna/Bridgeman Art Library
P 131 (bottom)	Portrait of Henry VIII (c. 1525-30) English School (16th century) Philip Mould Historical Portraits Ltd, London/Bridgeman Art Library
P 132	Arthur, Prince of Wales, Mary Evans Picture Library
P 133	A banquet in the Presence Chamber, Hampton Court, Joseph Nash, *The Mansions of England in the Olden Time*, Mary Evans Picture Library
P 134	Windsor Castle, *Gentleman's Magazine*, Mary Evans Picture Library
P 135	Picnic during a royal hunt, from Turbervile's *The Noble Art of Venerie or Hunting*, Mary Evans Picture Library
P 136	Jester in cap and bells, A Kohl, Mary Evans Picture Library

Portrait, supposed to be of Catherine of Aragon, painted by Michiel Sittow in 1503/4.

Portrait of Henry VIII painted in the mid-1520s.

Stained glass portrait of Arthur, Prince of Wales, Catherine of Aragon's first husband. Arthur died in 1502 within a few months of his wedding. Catherine married his younger brother, Henry, in 1509.

A banquet in the Presence Chamber of Hampton Court Palace.

A view of Windsor Castle during the reign of Henry VIII's daughter, Elizabeth I.

An engraving showing a picnic during a royal hunt in the sixteenth century.

A jester wearing a traditional costume with cap and bells.

ANNE BOLEYN AND ME

Richmond Palace, 1525

13th August 1525

This is the diary of Elinor Valjean, aged eleven.

Today is my sister Rosanna's birthday. Mama gave her a beautiful diary to write in, because Rosanna is sixteen, the same age as Mama was when she came to England with Catherine of Aragon, our queen. I am going to write a diary as well, only I do not have a proper one, so I have to write it on scraps of paper. I will keep them in the back of my Latin book, so they will be private.

I am not jealous of Rosanna. Of course she must have nice things for her birthday. I gave her a beaded cap that I'd sewn myself, with some help from Mama. But I will have to wait a long time before I am sixteen, and I want to start writing my diary now. Mama began hers because she was leaving Spain and going on a dangerous sea voyage to a strange country. She showed Rosanna and me her diary, with its close-packed lines of neat Spanish writing. Mine will not look like that. I keep trying to make my writing smaller and more tidy, but I never seem to manage it.

Papa would laugh if he knew about my diary pages. He isn't unkind, but he laughs at everything. I suppose it is because he is the court jester, "Mr John", as they call him. He says he has to remember that things are funny because if he starts to think they are serious or sad, he would lose his job. I want to be a jester, too, but I am a girl, so I have to wear long dresses that make it hard to jump and tumble as he does. I wish I had been a boy. My brothers have far more fun, learning archery and fighting with swords and quarter-staves. Little William is not much good at it yet, being only four and not very strong, but Daniel, at seven, thinks himself quite the man.

Mama reminds me that I am lucky. She and Queen Catherine were childhood friends, so we live as members of the royal court, in whichever palace King Henry VIII chooses to have his household. Mama and Papa both serve the King and Queen, he as the jester and she as Catherine's friend and favourite lady, and we children will be royal servants when we are old enough. Meanwhile, we ourselves are served by a great army of people who work in the barns and the yards and the smoky kitchens, tending livestock, washing clothes, and preparing and serving food.

Yes, we are lucky. We do not put in long hours of work in the fields, digging and sowing and reaping. We do not cart dung or pick stones or undertake the horrible work of slaughtering and skinning and plucking. Our food arrives ready-cooked, served on gold dishes if the King is entertaining guests. We play music and sing and dance, and every summer we go with the royal party on progress to other parts of the country while the palace where we have spent the winter is cleaned. When we come back in the autumn, we find the soot gone from the walls and the grease and filth scrubbed off the floors. There are fresh rushes scattered in the dining hall, sweet to tread on, and the bed-linen is washed and aired. I always love those first weeks after our return, while all the rooms still smell clean.

I would not have chosen to be a girl, but I enjoy some very nice things that the boys do not share. Sometimes Mama lets me join her when she and Maria de Salinas spend afternoons with the Queen. They talk together in Spanish, which I understand though I am not good at writing it, and they do their fine embroidery. Mostly it is Spanish style, black on white, as richly patterned as the bright sparkle of sunshine through dark leaves. It is very beautiful, but secretly I prefer the English use of reds and purples, blues and browns and gold. The Queen has all these colours, though she seldom uses them, and I love arranging the hanks of silk like a rainbow in their lacquered box. Queen Catherine said I could. She is a wonderful lady. Although she is the Queen of England, she is so kind.

I wish I was better at embroidery. I try hard, but my fingers seem sticky and awkward, and the thread makes itself into grubby knots. Perhaps I will find it easier when I am older. Meanwhile, I am always glad if Papa comes to join us, playing his lute or viol for the Queen and telling funny rhymes, for then I can lay the work down and listen. He can only be with us if King Henry does not need his services, for, like everyone else in the court, he has to obey orders.

This morning he could not come. To my amazement, Queen Catherine asked me to play instead, and handed me her own lute. I was very nervous, but she smiled, and when I had finished she clapped her hands.

Papa must have told her I can dance as well, and that I make up my own stories, for she asked me to do these things, and afterwards she laughed and applauded again. She said I take after my father.

It was the greatest compliment she could pay me, for I would love to be like him. My brother Daniel would laugh if he knew I wanted to be a jester, and little William would laugh as well without understanding why. Even Mama and Rosanna might be shocked, so I never mention it. But I dream of it all the same, and then I feel warm and excited inside.

I must be careful not to get married, or I will never do anything but work as a wife and mother. Some girls have their first baby when they are only twelve, specially if they belong to the titled families. They could never be jesters, poor things.

Princesses have no say in choosing their husbands. The Queen's daughter, Princess Mary, is nine years old, two years younger than I am, but she was betrothed when she was six to the Holy Roman Emperor Charles V, who is a grown-up man. He is the Queen's nephew, so I should not be rude about him – but he is such a funny-looking person. I saw him when he came here for the betrothal ceremony, and he has a long, pointed chin that sticks out so he can hardly close his mouth. He belongs to the Habsburg family, and Mama says all of them look rather like that. Mary was sent off to Ludlow Castle last month, with a huge retinue of horses and servants, to live in a separate household there. I don't know why.

I must stop writing now. Mama is calling. She wants me to get

William ready for bed. I tell him a story every night, and he will not go to sleep without it.

14th August 1525

Rosanna told me why Princess Mary went to live in Ludlow Castle. It's all to do with the King's son, Henry Fitzroy. He is six years old, and his mother is not Queen Catherine, she is called Bessie Blount. The little boy was brought here to Richmond Palace in June, and there was a big ceremony while the King made him Duke of Richmond and Somerset. Then he was sent to the north of England to be head of a great household. Rosanna says the Queen was annoyed because her own daughter, Mary, had not been given any such honours, and she told Henry she was not pleased. In fact, there was a frightful argument between them. So Mary has now been given her own household, to be equal with her half-brother.

I hope she will like it. I would hate to be sent away from my home and family to a castle near Wales, which they say is a very wet place. Thank goodness I am not a princess.

I saw Mark Smeaton catch Rosanna by her waist yesterday and give her a kiss. She was very offended and pushed him away. Mark said he was only trying to wish her a happy birthday, but I don't think she believed it. Mark is one of the court musicians. He plays the lute well and has a good voice, but Rosanna detests him. "He is pathetic," she said. "Like a trodden-on spaniel, always hoping people will like him. He has no spirit. He is just cheeky, and that is a different thing." I didn't understand what she meant. I quite like Mark. He gave me a bit of sugar candy the other day.

The King was in high good humour this morning. I saw him run his hand down Anne Boleyn's back as she went through a door ahead of him yesterday, then he laughed and bent his head to kiss her on the cheek. Anne works with Mama and Rosanna as one of the Queen's ladies, but she does not seem to mind being kissed. She smiled up at the King, all gaiety. She has been away at Hever Castle, her parents' home, for the last two years, and only came back quite recently. Rosanna says the King himself is in love with her, and he sent her away because she was having an affair with a young man called Henry Percy. There was quite a rumpus about it, and Cardinal Wolsey, the King's close adviser, told Percy that Anne Boleyn was not a suitable wife for a young man of good family. Percy was sent off to marry someone else. And Rosanna says Thomas Wyatt, the poet, is in love with Anne now.

I think all that is very silly. I love my family and I love the grey cat called Minna and the dogs that lie around when we all eat in the great hall, waiting for bones and scraps to be thrown. I love horses, too. But poets and young men called Percy sound a terrible bore.

This afternoon the King's mood changed completely, and he flew into one of his rages. Papa had a terrible time with him. King Henry loves music and plays well himself, so he is usually easy to amuse, but today something had upset him. Papa found out later that the Emperor Charles has broken off his engagement to Mary. The King has taken it as a personal insult, so his temper has been explosive ever since the news came. The whole court was tiptoeing about for fear of being shouted at, and even the Queen, who is always so calm and wise, dissolved into tears.

2nd October 1525

I meant to write my diary every day, but there are so many other things to do. I practise my dancing and singing, and Papa has given me a wooden flute, so that is a new instrument to learn, as well as the viol and lute. But I love the sound it makes, and Papa is a good teacher. My fingers are getting quicker at finding the notes.

Mark Smeaton still pesters Rosanna, though she won't have anything to do with him, and Thomas Wyatt gazes with soulful eyes at Anne Boleyn. But so does the King, which I find very odd. If she is too common a girl for young Percy to marry, how can she cast her spell on the King of England? Everyone is whispering that he is in love with her, but I can't understand it. King Henry is married to Queen Catherine, so how can he be in love with Anne? I am sure the Queen must be very upset about it. I asked Mama, and she sighed and said, "Poor lady – if only she had given him a son."

It is true that the Queen was unlucky. She had child after child, but all of them died except Mary. I know babies die sometimes. Mama had a little boy after I was born, and he died before he was a year old. But at least she has four of us. People say the Queen's last childbirth left her injured, so she cannot have any more children. The King is disappointed because he wanted a son who would inherit the throne of England. All this fuss about sons puzzles me. Surely Princess Mary can be Queen of England when King Henry dies? Her grandmother, Isabella, was Queen of Spain, and she ruled the country, with some help from her husband. If Isabella could do it, why not Mary? Mama shook her head when I suggested this. "King Henry is set on having a son," she said.

15th February 1526

There was a joust this afternoon. We watched from the covered stand, and Daniel was grumbling that he is not old enough yet to take part. I said, "But you will one day." He is lucky. I myself will always be sitting on the benches under the striped awning, a mere spectator.

When the men rode in, they looked magnificent, as they always do. They were in armour, of course, but scarlet plumes flew from their helmets, and they wore full-skirted, embroidered tunics. Their horses were beautifully dressed as well, in embroidered trappings that covered them almost completely, just showing the lower part of their legs. There was one I specially liked, in pale blue and silver.

When the King came riding in on his big, black horse, a murmur went up because his tunic was stitched with the words, DECLARE I DARE NOT. All the ladies were giggling behind their hands, and I asked Mama what it meant. Her face had turned quite pink and she said, "Never mind," so I asked Rosanna later. She told me the words meant the King has a new love, but he dares not say her name. But everyone knows her name. It is Anne Boleyn.

I keep thinking about Anne, wondering what it must be like to be loved by a king who already has a wife. I came face to face with her this evening as she brought a flask of sweet wine to the Queen's chamber. She is hardly taller than I am, a slender wisp of a thing. I suppose I must have been staring because she asked me what I thought I was looking at. She sounded very annoyed. It was no use pretending I hadn't been looking. I dropped her a respectful curtsey while I thought fast, then said, "I was looking at you."

"And why, pray?" she asked.

I told her, "Because you are so beautiful." Papa has always said a jester must look innocent.

It worked very well. "Bless the child," Anne said. She patted my cheek and smiled at me. Then she went on to the Queen's door with her flask of wine.

She is not really beautiful. She has a slim figure, but her face is very pale, with a pointed chin. Rosanna says she is quick-witted, with a ready retort to any courtier who makes a flirtatious remark, and the men like her for that. She has jet-black eyes, as lively as a bird's. She makes me think of a magpie; neat and smart and attracted to things that glitter. And I suppose the greatest and most glittering prize of them all must be the King.

19th April 1526

King Henry hurled a jug of wine at Papa today, causing him a deep cut above the eyebrow. Mama said nothing, just bathed the wound and put some knitbone ointment on it. This afternoon we heard that Henry has sent Thomas Wyatt away to Italy on some sort of diplomatic mission that will last for years. Rosanna laughed and said, "His Majesty must be getting desperate. He is not used to having his wishes refused."

Mama looked at her and shook her head. Neither of them would explain what Rosanna meant. But I met Mark Smeaton coming from the Queen's chamber with his lute, and I asked him. He was happy to tell me. "The King wants Anne to be his mistress, and she has turned him down. So he is raging about like a mad bull."

I know what a mistress is. It is a woman who lives with a man as if the pair of them were married, only they are not. I am glad Anne has refused to do that. It would be dreadful for Queen Catherine.

Mark laughed when I said this. "Anne has no sympathy for the Queen," he said. "She is refusing to be the King's mistress for just one reason. She wants to be his wife, and she will settle for nothing less."

That is nonsense, of course. Henry is married to Queen Catherine, and the Church does not allow marriage vows to be broken. They will be man and wife for ever.

23rd August 1526

Mama says I am a woman now. I was frightened when I found traces of blood and ran to her because I thought I was ill, but she told me it's a very important part of growing up. I felt angry at first. Couldn't I have had a choice about whether I wanted to grow up? I have always wanted to have the same freedom as my brothers, to run about and ride and shoot, but Mama shook her head today, and said women have more important things to do. Perhaps it will not be too bad. The ladies of the court ride horses and fly hawks and go hunting, I suppose. In any case, I cannot change my life, any more than I can stop the winds blowing or the sun shining, so I will enjoy whatever there is to enjoy.

Rosanna has fallen in love with Diego Luiz de Frontera, the son of one of the Spanish attendants who came over from Granada with the Queen. She blushes and says it is not serious, but she cannot keep her eyes off him. He is very handsome, slim and broad-shouldered, with dark hair and eyes. I can see she is very happy.

Poor Princess Mary will not be happy. The French king, Francis I, wants to marry again because his wife died two years ago, and he has offered his hand as a husband for Mary. King Henry is delighted and so is Cardinal Wolsey.

The Queen, however, is not delighted at all. The French have always been enemies of Spain, so she does not want her daughter to marry their king. Besides, Mary is still only ten, and Francis is even older than the Emperor Charles. He could be her grandfather.

20th February 1527

Today is my thirteenth birthday – and I have been appointed a Lady of Court, to wait on the Queen! In a way it is nothing new, as I have always helped Rosanna and Mama, but I feel very grown-up, with my hair braided neatly under an embroidered cap, a present from Rosanna. Mama gave me a new gown, much more elaborate than any of my childhood dresses, and although I have always preferred boyish things, I must admit, this lovely dress is a pleasure. I specially like the slashed and embroidered over-sleeves that show the brocaded fabric underneath. They can be changed if they become soiled, as they are easier to clean than an entire gown. Mama gave me three pairs of sleeves, but my favourites are the pale-green silk ones, embroidered in blue and silver-white.

How strange it is to feel like a court lady! Suddenly I am included in the gossip instead of being sent away like a little girl, and I am starting to understand how things are done. People who want a favour of the King used to ask Queen Catherine to put in a word for them, but now they ask Anne Boleyn instead, knowing she is the one Henry listens to.

The Queen ignores all this. Since Christmas I have been going out with her and some other ladies almost every day, helping her to distribute charity among the crowds who flock to see her. Whatever her private worries may be, she is always serene and kind, and the common people adore her. They have probably heard the rumours about Anne, for gossip can never be stopped, but it has merely made them more protective of their true queen.

10th April 1527

We have been at Hampton Court all through the winter. I love this place. The frosty daylight shines in through all its great windows, and it is a joy to walk through its grounds and see the spring flowers blooming.

A delegation is here from France to talk about Mary's marriage to the French king. Their ambassador said an extraordinary thing. He asked whether Mary really is the King's legitimate daughter. The courtiers who were listening dared not even glance at each other, they were so embarrassed. How can anyone doubt that Mary is the child of Henry and Catherine of Aragon?

Rosanna explained later what the ambassador meant. Apparently the King is trying to claim that he was never legally married to Catherine. He has found a passage in the Bible that says it is unlawful for a man to marry his brother's wife – and Catherine was of course married to Henry's elder brother, Arthur, for a few months. Arthur then died, and Catherine waited for years before it was decided that she could marry Henry, who had always been her true love.

Everything has changed now. Henry is trying to wriggle out of his marriage so he can take Anne as his new wife. And the only way he can do this is to declare his marriage to Queen Catherine illegal. I have never seen Mama so furious. "What a way to treat her!" she fumed. "And after all she has done for him! She ran the country while he was away at his silly war with France, she beat the Scots, she has advised him wisely for all these years, she has brought him the love of the people – and he will throw all this away for some obstinate girl who will not give in to him? The man is insane!"

17th April 1527

Cardinal Wolsey has assured the French that Mary is indeed the King's rightful daughter. I am glad. But I still do not want her to marry that old man.

Meanwhile, there is scandalous news. King Henry has asked Anne Boleyn to be his wife! How *can* he? Obviously he thinks he can dissolve his marriage to Catherine, but that is hardly the point. His determination to marry Anne astounds everyone. He has had mistresses before, many of them – we are all used to that – but to take this girl as a *wife* seems extraordinary. She is no more than a court servant, like the rest of us. Her family has distant royal connections, but whose has not? My own family cannot be called aristocratic – after all, we are not even English. But Mama is from a titled Spanish family, and her uncle was for many years the Spanish ambassador. Anne's father married Elizabeth Howard, of an old titled family, but he himself came of tradesmen. The whole court is buzzing with speculation about what will happen next.

2nd May 1527

The betrothal between Mary and the French king has been agreed. There was a banquet last night, and the dancing and drinking went on long afterwards. When the King was dancing with his daughter, he suddenly pulled off Mary's jewelled cap and let the wavy length of her fair hair fall free, as if to show off her beauty. Everyone laughed and applauded. Poor Mary, though. I would not be in her place, bound to marry an old man whom she has never met.

17th May 1527

King Henry and Cardinal Wolsey are meeting at Westminster with William Warham, the Archbishop of Canterbury, to talk about the King's marriage. Henry wants Cardinal Wolsey to put the question to the Pope for his decision, but the Cardinal was horrified at the whole idea. He cannot refuse the King's request, though. Nobody can refuse the King anything – except the Pope, of course.

Tonight I asked Mama what it says in the Bible about a man who marries his brother's wife. She took down our own Bible and turned to Leviticus, and ran her finger down the pages. We stared at the close-printed lines by the candle's light. Most of the chapters were about sacrifice and burnt offerings, but then she came to the rules by which a man must live if he is to be pure. "This is it," she said. We read the words of chapter 20, verse 21 together:

> *Qui duxerit uxorem fratris sui, rem facit illicitam, turpitudinem fratris sui revelavit absque liberis sunt.*
>
> *And if a man shall take his brother's wife, it is an unclean thing; he hath uncovered his brother's nakedness; they shall be childless.*

"You see?" Mama said. "Henry thinks he has sinned in marrying Catherine, who was his brother's wife. And he fears that God's punishment for that is to deny him a son."

I found the whole chapter very frightening. It showed a fierce and unforgiving God, greedy for blood and the smoke of burnt meat. Then I was scared again, this time by my own dislike of it. After all, the Bible is holy. We do not have the choice to believe or not believe. As a mere human being, I dare not imagine how the Lord God will judge our king, who only started to fear that he had sinned when his desires were moving elsewhere.

2nd June 1527

The Pope is in prison! Emperor Charles has been campaigning in Italy, and last month his soldiers went on a mutinous rampage and sacked the city of Rome. The men were unpaid and starving, we hear, but all the same it seems a terrible thing to do. The Holy Father is locked up in a fortress called Castel San Angelo, and the Emperor has done nothing to free him, merely apologized. We all think he has lost control of his army.

Papa laughed when he heard. "So the King is out of luck!" he said. While Pope Clement remains imprisoned, he cannot judge on the question of Henry Tudor's marriage. And Henry cannot marry Anne until the Pope agrees that his previous marriage is ended.

The King is furious, of course. If the Pope cannot give a judgement on his case, then somebody must. He is sending Wolsey to France to set up a ruling council with the other cardinals in Avignon. Can they really act without Pope Clement's authority? Most people think it is impossible, but preparations have started for Wolsey's departure. George Cavendish will be with the party, and he is rushing about like a man demented, organizing horses and mules, baggage and equipment.

Mama is equally busy with the provision of black velvet coats for the clerical gentlemen who will go with the Cardinal, and we are all stitching frantically, even I who am no kind of needlewoman compared with Mama. At least I can sew a straight seam nowadays. Anne Boleyn herself sews with us, and her fingers are very quick and neat. Until this business is decided, she remains one of the Queen's ladies, of no more importance than the rest of us. But of course everyone watches her, and malicious gossip abounds.

6th June 1527

Henry has sent Anne away to her parents' home in Hever. I suppose he feels it is time to remove her from being no more than a serving lady.

22nd June 1527

King Henry went to see Catherine today, and asked her to release him and retire from being queen.

Heavens, what a rumpus! The Queen wept like a thing demented, and screamed at him that she was and always would be his legal wife.

Henry emerged from her chambers looking ruffled and angry. I do not feel much sympathy for him. From what Mama has told me, Catherine went through years of hardship and neglect before he married her, and she would rather die than let him cast her off. She is sending a messenger to ask her nephew, the Emperor Charles, if he will help her. Since Charles is responsible for imprisoning the Pope, he can presumably talk to him and perhaps persuade him not to dissolve her marriage. The messenger is one of Catherine's most trusted servants, a man named Felipez.

24th June 1527

Henry found out about the messenger. I expect one of Anne Boleyn's supporters told him. He sent riders galloping after the man all the way to Dover, but when they got there Felipez was already aboard a ship that had sailed. So the Emperor will get to hear of his aunt's plight. I cannot imagine that he will do much about it, though. He is too busy fighting wars.

16th July 1527

The question of Henry's marriage has come to the notice of the English Parliament as well as to the Church. Thomas More, the Lord Chancellor, has told the King his marriage cannot be called illegal. John Fisher, the Bishop of Rochester, has said the same thing. Henry is not pleased.

15th September 1527

The French ambassadors are here for more negotiations about Mary's marriage. It was a state occasion, so Henry and Catherine sat side by side to watch a masque performed by children, smiling as though nothing could be wrong between them. They still look a handsome couple, though both of them are bulkier in the body than they once were. I think they are still fond of each other, for Henry visits his wife in her chambers quite often. Perhaps this business about Anne will blow over. I hope so.

16th December 1527

The Pope has been freed. Nobody knows whether the Emperor spoke to him on Catherine's behalf, and meanwhile King Henry has sent his secretary, William Knight, to Rome. They say he bears a message asking His Holiness to declare that Henry may marry any other woman, providing his marriage to Catherine is annulled.

Cardinal Wolsey is back from his meeting with the Cardinals in Avignon, having achieved nothing. As the King's closest adviser, he does not expect Henry to send messages to the Pope without consulting him, and he looks very displeased.

1st January 1528

On this New Year's morning, Rosanna was married to her true love, Diego Luiz de Frontera, in the chapel here at Greenwich. Mama wept tears of happiness, and then she turned to me and said, "God willing, you will be next, Ellie."

I am nearly fourteen, well old enough to be married, but I still find it hard to take the idea seriously. There are constant flirtations among the courtiers, and I suppose it would be easy enough to show an interest in one of them, but they are so much the same as each other – well-dressed, amusing, expert in all the graces of court life, and delighting in malicious gossip. I can see why Mama married my father, a Frenchman who lived by his own skills and had no real respect for any of them. And why should I hurry? I enjoy my music, and play often for the Queen now – even for the King sometimes, though his changing moods can be alarming.

As for Rosanna – she looked lovely, in a gown of white silk sewn with small pearls, and her dark hair loose. With Diego beside her, handsome in an embroidered doublet of black velvet, she seemed utterly blissful. They will have their own room now, but they go on serving the Queen in the same way. Does marriage really make such a difference? Yes, perhaps it does – but I still find it hard to imagine.

24th February 1528

The Pope has agreed to let Wolsey and one other cardinal hear the King's case against Queen Catherine in England. The other cardinal will be Lorenzo Campeggio, who has to come from Rome. They say the poor man suffers dreadfully from gout, so his journey is likely to be a slow and painful one. The case will not be heard for a while, so perhaps the weather will be kinder by the time he sets out.

At Henry's command, Wolsey has made a public announcement about "the King's great matter", as it is being called. The common people in the cities and the countryside now know that their king is seeking to escape from his marriage to Catherine. But their loyalty is to the Queen. I was with her this afternoon when she rode out, and all along the way crowds gathered to wish her success over her enemies. Henry is scowling and angry. Mama says he fears that Catherine will stir up a rebellion against him. In the early days of their marriage he often turned to her for advice on what he should do, and he knows she is clear-minded and politically astute. She would do nothing to harm him, though. He is her husband and her lord, and she loves him.

4th June 1528

The sweating sickness has come to London. It is a bad outbreak, and everyone is thrown into a panic. The King is very afraid of this disease. I suppose because it killed his brother, Arthur. He has ordered that we must be ready to leave at any moment.

14th June 1528

One of the court ladies has fallen ill with the sickness, so we will leave tomorrow. Anne is still with her parents at Hever, so she at least will be safe. I do not know where the rest of us will go, but we are frantically packing.

15th June 1528

Papa is ill. When we got up early this morning, he was shivering, although his skin was burning hot. He tried to tell us it was nothing serious, but his teeth chattered as he spoke, and it was obvious that he could not manage two days of riding. Mama will stay with him, but I have been ordered to go with the royal party. Diego and Rosanna will be with us as well. I am scribbling this quickly, as we are almost ready to leave. My poor parents – I am frantic with worry about both of them.

17th June 1528

We are in a place called Tittenhanger, in Hertfordshire, at the house of the Abbot of St Albans. The King thinks we will be safe from the sickness here. My mind is constantly with Mama and Papa, left behind to cope as best they can. A lot of the servants are still there, so at least somebody will fetch water and food for them, but I am full of fear.

23rd June 1528

A rider arrived in the middle of last night to tell the King that Anne Boleyn has the sickness, but then he added the terrible, casual words, "And I regret to say Michel Valjean has expired. Your good jester, sire."

I burst into tears. The other ladies took me out of the room and tried to comfort me. One of them ran for Rosanna and told her, and we wept together. She has Diego, though, so she is not alone with her grief. It is late now, and the candle is almost burned out, but I cannot stop weeping. Papa seems so real in my mind, with his thin, lively face, but I will never see him again, never watch his quick fingers over the lute strings, never laugh at his wit, never marvel at a new story. The messenger said my mother was somewhat ill with the same sickness but is now recovering. I thank the good Lord for that – to lose her as well would be too much to bear.

Rosanna did what she could to comfort me. Papa has been spared the pains of old age, she pointed out. He will not suffer stiffness of the joints and toothache and the slow loss of his sight as most people do. This is true, and I suppose I am merely selfish in my constant weeping. The loss of my dear father is like an injury to my spirit, and the soreness of it goes on and on.

28th June 1528

We hear that Anne Boleyn's attack was only a slight one, though her sister's husband, William Carey, died of the sickness. Anne had the best of attention. Henry's own doctor was out tending the sick, but he sent Dr Butts to her at once. This morning he despatched a rider with a haunch of venison to assist her recovery.

We are packing to go back to London, but it will be a sad return.

2nd August 1528

We arrived back yesterday. Mama and I wept together. The room she shared with Papa seems so empty now. I wish I could have said a better goodbye to him than the few rushed words before we had to leave.

Anne Boleyn is no longer in the Queen's service. King Henry has given her an apartment of her own, a small place off the tiltyard in Greenwich Palace, where he may see her whenever he chooses. Mama, in the midst of her own grief, is outraged at this new insult to the Queen.

9th October 1528

Cardinal Campeggio arrived today, after two months of travelling. I thought there would be a big reception for him, as he is to assist Wolsey in deciding on the question of the King's marriage, but this was not the case. He came into London by way of the river, on a barge that had no special decoration, and took to his bed at once.

Such a long journey must have been agony for a man who suffers from gout.

It is more than three months since Papa died, but I still miss him. I feel that I shall never be light-hearted again.

13th October 1528

Queen Catherine spoke to me kindly today. "Your father would not want to see you so sad, Elinor," she said. My eyes filled with tears again, but she told me something I had never thought of. "Every woman carries grief," she said. "It is like a fire, painful at first. But when you become used to it, you will find it a source of strength." I thought of how much grief she has known in her life, and made her a deep curtsey. "God go with you," she said, and blessed me.

24th October 1528

Wolsey and Campeggio came to see Catherine today. I know now that they wanted her to enter a nunnery so that Henry would be free to marry Anne, and she refused, but at the time I only heard the raised voices and the anger. The two men came out looking red-faced and annoyed, and went off to report their failure to the King.

I would not be in their shoes. Henry's temper has been more than usually short lately, as he is troubled by an injury to his leg, the result of a fall from his horse in the summer. The wound is ulcerated and will not heal, and he hates to be less than perfectly fit and healthy.

29th October 1528

A letter was brought to the Queen this afternoon. She said nothing when she read it, but she looked very distressed. Mama told me afterwards that it came from the Privy Council. They have advised the King to separate himself from Catherine completely. They have also told him he should remove Princess Mary from her company.

12th November 1528

King Henry did a strange thing today. He threw open Bridewell Palace and invited the common people to come in. And in they came, of course, with their smelly clothes and dirty faces, their baskets and bundles and babies and dogs, staring about them at the rich hangings and the gilded ceiling. The King entered and stood before the throne, wearing his robes of state. He told them of his need to have a son who would rule England after him, then he spoke warmly of Catherine. Were he to have his time over again, he said, he would marry no other – but he had to think of the future. He explained his case for taking a new wife, and the people stared at him in a mixture of respect and astonishment. Some of them nodded as he spoke, and at the end there were shouts of "God Save the King!" But there were sideways glances among them as they were ushered down the steps and back into the street.

Not even Henry himself can make them like Anne Boleyn. She is too close to their own common blood to command their respect. Going out among the last of them, I heard one woman murmur to another, "She is nothing but a scheming harlot." And there are many at court who would agree.

15th November 1528

This is a dreadful day. The King has commanded that I must leave the Queen's service and join Anne Boleyn's household. He is moving her from Greenwich to a much grander house in the Strand, with a garden that runs down to the river. She has demanded that most of the younger ladies shall wait upon her, and I am among them. Rosanna was not chosen, so I will not even have the company of my sister.

I am full of resentment. It is a bitter thing to have to serve a fellow servant, no matter how she has risen in the world. I will have to leave Mama, too, for she, like Rosanna and Diego, will stay with the Queen.

The poor Queen – her chambers will seem empty and dull without so many of the lively girls who have been like a family to her. She is 43 now, the same age as Mama. Maria de Salinas is still with her, but she is far older. A staff of new ladies will be chosen by Wolsey and the King, and I know what that means. Their function will be to spy on the Queen and report back to their masters on whatever she says and does. I am glad Rosanna and Mama will be with her, even though I shall miss them.

I almost regret the years spent learning my music and dancing, and the gaiety of heart that led me to laugh and make up stories. Look where it has led me! But I seem to hear Papa assuring me that music lasts longer than people do. He is right, of course. I will take up my lute and play for my own comfort, for there is no other.

Christmas 1528

After a few weeks at the Strand house, we have come here to Greenwich Palace for the Christmas period. My lady Anne is housed in separate quarters from the rest of the court, and we are perpetually busy, providing refreshments and entertaining her constant stream of visitors. The Queen is in a different part of the palace (with Mama and Rosanna, thank goodness) and she appears with the King when guests are invited, to give the impression that things are continuing as normal. I do not see much of these occasions, for I have to play and sing as commanded by Her Ladyship. My spirit of goodwill is sadly lacking.

8th January 1529

Christmas is over, and I am back at the house in the Strand. When I picked up one of Mistress Anne's discarded dresses this morning I found under it a book by Simon Fish, called *The Supplication of Beggars*. I looked into its pages, and saw that it was in favour of the Bible being translated into English so that any common person may read it. They say Mr Fish had to leave the country, and I am not surprised. To write such a thing is rank heresy. I made the sign of the cross and returned the book to its place. Latin has always been the language of religion. What will happen to the authority of the Church if people start to take the mysteries of God into their own hands? The Pope will surely never allow it.

The people of England are forbidden to read heretical books, yet the King does not mind Anne flaunting them under his nose. Even worse, he reads them himself. There is one called *The Obedience of a Christian Man, and How Kings Ought to Govern*, by William Tynedale. I picked it up from beside Henry's chair the other day, knowing nothing of its contents. Then I found that Mr Tyndale has actually translated the Bible into English! What's more, he says a ruling monarch should have authority over the Church in his country – he need not bow to the authority of the Pope. No wonder King Henry finds it interesting. If he could make himself head of the English Church, he would not have to ask permission from Rome to divorce his wife.

18th February 1529

Nobody will take the responsibility of deciding on the King's case against Catherine. Campeggio now says he is not empowered to make any judgement without referring to the Pope – and the Pope is ill, we hear, and unable to attend to any questions at all. Henry banged his fist on the table when he heard about this. He is furiously impatient, and although my sympathies are for the Queen, I can see how he feels. These endless delays are unbearable.

20th February 1529

Today is my fifteenth birthday. I have not told anyone here, for I have no particular friends. I wish so much that I could have stayed in Greenwich, with all my family together as we were at Christmas.

When the daily rider came from there this morning with messages for Anne, he gave me letters from Mama and Rosanna, and some exciting packages. Daniel sent me a bird he had carved from a piece of wood, and little William had wrapped up a pomegranate. From Mama I had a pair of gloves, intricately worked with her beautiful embroidery, and Rosanna – dear Rosanna! – sent me a diary. She put a letter in with it, saying she thought I might like to write things down, now I am on my own in this place. "A diary is not as good as a friend," she said, "but it can help if there are times when you are lonely."

She is quite right, of course. I wonder if she knows I have been keeping a diary all this time. My disused Latin book bulges now with the bits of paper I have tucked into it. I think I will copy them all into my new, proper diary. It will be something to do in the dark evenings, and my writing is neater now than it was when I was eleven. Mama's letter said the Queen sends her good wishes for my birthday. I was very thrilled by that.

She went on to say the Queen knows of a document written by the old Pope Julius II, who was alive many years ago when Catherine was married to Henry's brother, Arthur. Arthur died only six months after their marriage, and the Pope's document was written to give Catherine permission to marry Henry. This means Henry cannot possibly say his marriage to Catherine was illegal. It proves absolutely that the Queen is his true wife, and has every right to remain so.

There are difficulties, though. The document is now in Spain. It was among the papers of my great-uncle, Rodrigo De Puebla, and when he died everything was returned to his home country to be looked after by the Emperor Charles. The Queen needs to have it in her own hands, of course, but Henry will not want her to possess such a powerful piece of evidence. If the Emperor sends the document to England, Catherine fears it will be conveniently lost. Mama says she is hoping her nephew, the Emperor, will think of something.

27th March 1529

Although Anne likes to hear me play and sing, she does not confide in me at all. I can hardly blame her – she must know I still love Queen Catherine. But her other ladies gossip, even though they have been picked for their loyalty to Anne, so I hear a lot about the Queen's "obstructive attitude", as they call it, and the irritating inactivity of the Pope.

The Holy Father is said to be recovering from his illness, but he is perhaps not fully in charge of things yet for he has agreed that Wolsey and Campeggio may call a court at Westminster for a hearing of "the King's great matter". They have been given the power to judge on the Pope's behalf. Anne and her friends are delighted, naturally. They are sure the case will go against Catherine, and Henry will then be free to marry Anne. I do not share their certainty. The Queen is a shrewd and determined fighter, and the people of England are on her side.

All the same, things are difficult for her. Mama's last letter says the Emperor listened to her request about the old Pope's document. Understanding that the original might be intercepted and destroyed, he sent a *copy* of it to London, but ensured that it was signed by the most eminent bishops in Spain, testifying that it was a genuine reproduction of the original. Surely that should have been good enough? But when Henry and Wolsey saw it, they at once dismissed it as a forgery.

20th May 1529

The cardinals' court really is going to take place in Westminster. We have to move my lady Anne's household to Hever for the duration of the hearing, as the King feels she should be away from London. I have little time to write – there is so much to be packed and organized. Anne is agitated and upset, saying she wants to stay here. She seems deeply nervous about the hearing. She knows how warmly the people regard their queen, and knows too that if the case goes in Catherine's favour that will be the end of her own hopes.

The Queen has chosen the lawyers who will defend her. They are the bishops of Ely and St Asaph, old Archbishop Warham of Canterbury, and her faithful friend John Fisher, Bishop of Rochester. They sound impressive – but the King may have even more important men on his side.

18th June 1529

Hever Castle is a lovely place. It looks forbidding from outside, with its sheer walls rising from a moat that runs all round it, but there are also beautiful gardens all around, and meadows that run down to the little river. They are full of buttercups and cow parsley, and there is no sound except for the birds singing. It is so good to be away from the noisy centre of London, with its clatter of hooves and constant rattle of wheels over cobblestones. The summer evenings are warm, and the scent of fresh-scythed hay is sweet. I am happy here.

So happy. I have met someone I love. His name is Tom Freeman. He was out with a couple of dogs early one morning when I was walking by the willow trees along the river. He smiled when he saw me and said, "Dabbling in the dew?"

I sang him a snatch of the old song as a reply: "Makes the milkmaids fair." And he joined in. He has a lovely voice, deep but very sweet, like dark honey.

We both laughed when the song came to an end. He has brown hair that curls like the coats of his retrievers, and his eyes are grey. He smiled and said he didn't usually burst into song with strangers. I said I didn't, either. I was wearing an old dress, and the hem was all wet with the dew on the long grass. I hadn't even braided my hair, and it was hanging loose down my back, but he didn't seem to mind. "Midsummer madness," he said. "The sun hardly above the trees, and here we stand, singing like a pair of cuckoos."

I said, "Cuckoos don't sing, they just cuckoo," and he said it probably sounded like song to them.

I wish we were a pair of cuckoos. I'd like to fly away with him, and leave this court and all its scheming people behind. He is the blacksmith here at Hever. Mostly he shoes the horses and doctors them for any injury or illness, but he makes things as well – cart-springs, gate hinges, tools for the farm workers. I went with him into the smithy where he works. It was very cool in there, as the forge fire was not lit. He kissed me. I never thought I would want a stranger to do that, but Tom does not seem like a stranger. I feel as if I have known him for ever.

I keep thinking about our meeting. I remember every word of what he said and what I said, and reliving it has warmed me all day. One of Anne's ladies looked at me and asked, "Why are you smiling?" I said I didn't know. My cuckoo morning is not for sharing with people who gossip so maliciously about each other, and would do about me as well, given half a chance.

21st July 1529

The King's case is being heard at Westminster. Riders come daily with messages for Madam Anne. Most of them are in Henry's bold hand, but today there was also a letter for me from Mama. Queen Catherine, she says, appeared just once before the court. She fell on her knees and made a passionate speech, declaring her love for Henry and her belief in the truth of her marriage. After that she left the court on the arm of one of her gentlemen, and has refused to return. They hope a judgement will be made in two days' time. I do hope so. And I hope they decide in favour of the Queen.

23rd July 1529

The trial has come to an end, but nothing has been decided. Campeggio shocked everyone by announcing that the Pope had changed his mind about allowing any cardinal to give judgement. The ruling would have to be considered in Rome. And the papal court in Rome always enjoyed a summer break of three months, so nothing further could be done until October. The King was so enraged that he stormed out of the court.

When Anne Boleyn read the letter that came from Henry this evening, her pale face flushed with fury. She said some extremely rude things about Campeggio. "And as to Wolsey, he is nothing more than a broken reed," she added. "Useless."

She has always hated Wolsey, but since receiving the letter, she has been pacing about in such a tempest of anger that none of us dares speak to her.

25th July 1529

Tom and I have met in the early morning for the last two days. I would like to see him more often, but the household is in a turmoil of packing and preparation, and I am frantically busy. The hearing at Westminster delayed our departure for the summer progress, and Anne is all impatience to set off. She is looking forward to it with special excitement, as Queen Catherine will be left behind this year. Henry has chosen to travel with Anne, parading her before the people as his chosen consort and maybe his future queen, so she is of course delighted.

Tom will be with us, thank goodness. King Henry has noticed that he cares for the horses well, and there is no time to send for his own blacksmith, who did not come with Anne's party to Hever. I am so glad!

14th August 1529

There is hardly time to write a word. We are constantly moving from one great house to another. Waltham Abbey, Barnet, Holborn, Windsor, Reading, Woodstock – there seems no end to the packing and unpacking. We will return to Greenwich in October, but meanwhile we are royal travellers, welcomed by our hosts wherever we go.

The common people are less enthusiastic. Anne, usually carried in a litter with the curtains drawn back so she can be seen, waves and smiles to them, but they do not smile back. Many of them scowl as our procession passes through their villages, and some shout abusive words, then duck away quickly before they can be seen and arrested. Their opinion is very clear. To them, Catherine is the only rightful queen.

20th September 1529

We are at Grafton in Northamptonshire, housed in a royal hunting lodge in the woods. Cardinal Campeggio came on a farewell visit to the King, as he has been recalled to Rome now that the fruitless trial is over. Wolsey arrived as well, but we were not instructed to prepare any accommodation for him. Campeggio was escorted to his quarters, but Wolsey was left standing in the courtyard on his own. Some of the ladies were secretly giggling, but I felt terribly sorry for the poor man. Fortunately, Sir Henry Norris came out and offered the Cardinal his own room.

This discourtesy is my lady Anne's doing, of course. Her loathing of Wolsey gets more and more intense. As if to make up for her rudeness, Henry asked Wolsey to meet with him and the Boleyn supporters later in the afternoon. I glimpsed the Cardinal going in through the door to the room where the Dukes of Suffolk, Norfolk and Rochester were assembled with others, and saw how he fell on his knees before the King. Henry put both his hands under Wolsey's elbows, helping him to rise. Then the door closed, cutting off my view.

I must go and help set the tables with gold plate and wine goblets. There is to be a great dinner tonight for Campeggio's departure. Henry has no cause to like him, but he will not neglect the proper courtesies.

21st September 1529

Anne Boleyn was sulky and out of humour all through the banquet yesterday evening, darting venomous glances at Wolsey and making slighting remarks. At one point Henry said to her in mock surprise, "I perceive you are not the Cardinal's friend." Anne retorted that she could not be Wolsey's friend, because he treated the King so badly. That is complete nonsense, of course. Wolsey would do anything for the King, and we all know it.

This morning she persuaded Henry to go hunting, just at the time when Wolsey and Campeggio had to depart. The King leaned down from his horse to bid them farewell, and spoke in warm terms, but it was a scant and inadequate way to take his leave of two eminent men.

4th October 1529

We are at Greenwich Palace, all of us together. It is so good to be with Mama and Rosanna and the boys again, for Queen Catherine is here, even though Henry spends most of his time with Anne. And Tom is to stay with us! He cured Anne's favourite horse when it went lame on progress, so she has demanded that he must be her personal blacksmith from now on. I thought her father might be annoyed, for he will not easily find another man with Tom's skills, but he made no objection. I suppose he has little choice but to fall in with his daughter's whims. If she marries the King, she will make her whole family rich and famous.

Henry is not troubled about such small matters as a new blacksmith, for he has a new cause for fury. His letters to Anne disappeared at the time when Campeggio left, and he is sure they were stolen. I heard him bellowing last night that the whole court is corrupt and he can trust nobody. But then, he had drunk a great amount of wine.

His mood improved this morning, after two men had been to see him. They spoke of Thomas Cranmer, a friend of theirs who has new ideas on the judgement of the King's case. This Cranmer contends that it does not have to be heard by the Pope or even by an assembly of cardinals. The clerics of England's own universities, he says, have the power to decide, and if the Archbishop of Canterbury should pronounce King Henry's marriage invalid, then invalid it is. When I heard this, my mind flew back to William Tynedale's book and the idea that the King can be head of the English Church. Perhaps Henry is thinking of it as well. He has commanded Cranmer to come and see him, and he seems much excited.

7th October 1529

The King has been in constant talks with Thomas Cranmer, who is now lodged at the house of Anne's father, Lord Rochford. Evidently his new friend has given him new ideas, for we hear that Henry intends to charge Cardinal Wolsey with something called praemunire. I asked one of the court gentlemen what it means, and he said it is the crime of asking a foreign power to judge on something that should be a nation's own business. I suppose this refers to the Pope's judgement on Henry's divorce. Rome is not England.

Cranmer, like Tynedale, seems to think the King can be his own judge, backed by the clerics of the English universities. It still sounds like heresy to me.

9th October 1529

King Henry has indeed charged Wolsey with praemunire. He has stripped him of his office as Lord Chancellor of England, and we are all stunned. The Cardinal himself is terribly upset. He has given almost all of his property to the King in an effort to placate him, including his great house called York Place, but the King remains adamant. Wolsey will retire to his one remaining home, a modest house in Esher, in Surrey.

Anne is delighted at his fall. I don't know why she hates Wolsey so much, but Rosanna tells me it is because of something that happened years ago, when Anne was in love with young Henry Percy. Even then, the King wanted her for himself, but he did not choose to say so. He left it to Wolsey to tell Anne she was not a suitable bride for a young man from a noble family and to pack her off to her parents at Hever. I think Wolsey did Anne a favour, for had she married Percy, she would have settled down with him and never dreamed of being the Queen of England – but she seems unconcerned about that. Wolsey slighted her, and she has never forgiven him. And at last she has had her revenge.

17th October 1529

A new Spanish ambassador has arrived. He is called Eustache Chapuys. He spent all morning in conference with Queen Catherine. Anne hates him. She knows an enemy when she sees one, and Chapuys has a hard, confident look about him. He is not impressed by Anne's influence with the King, and he does not mind what he says, either. Already he has been heard to refer to Anne Boleyn as "the concubine", which is a rather insulting way of referring to a man's mistress.

2nd November 1529

The King is delighted with Wolsey's house, York Place. He took Anne to see it on the very day it came into his hands. He is going to turn it into a palace for her, renaming it as Whitehall. Anne is ecstatic – but despite that, she still wants to see the Cardinal in prison or even executed. She nags Henry about it constantly, but without much success. The gift of the palace has calmed the King's temper, and he seems disinclined to punish Wolsey any further. He will allow him to keep his office as Archbishop of York, and Anne will have to be satisfied with her new house.

The place is already full of workmen making the necessary alterations. Anne wants to move in at once, not waiting for them to finish. She cannot wait to have her own court. Once installed in Whitehall, she will be queen in everything except name.

10th December 1529

What an upheaval it has been! We have all been working day and night to get everything exactly as my lady wants it.

Most of the time, she seems pleased with the way things are going, and so she should be, but there are occasional explosions of temper. She was enraged yesterday when she found out that Catherine still mends Henry's shirts. Anne herself is a good needlewoman, and she screamed protests at him.

Henry roared back at her on this occasion, but he does not seem seriously bothered by these outbursts. He continues to shower presents on her, and two days ago he honoured Anne's father with the title of Earl of Wiltshire. Her brother George becomes Viscount Rochford and Anne herself is to be known as the Lady Anne Boleyn – but she is not satisfied. She is impatient to become England's true queen, and she is careless of who listens as she argues with Henry. I heard her this very evening, shouting at him that she might by now be married to some other man, by whom she could have had children.

This was cruel of her. She knows how raw the King's feelings are on that subject – and after all, he is moving heaven and earth to try to make her his queen. It perplexes me that he thinks she is worth all this massive upheaval and trouble, but I suppose he loves her.

30th December 1529

News reaches us that Cardinal Wolsey is gravely ill. King Henry was saddened to hear it, for he and Wolsey are old friends, despite the differences that now part them. He said he would not lose him for £20,000. He gave orders for his own physician, Dr Butts, to attend the sick man, and in front of all of us he turned to Anne and told her she must send the Cardinal a token of her esteem. She did not argue, but meekly detached a tablet of gold from her belt and handed it to the King.

I thought she would resent being made to give such a valuable gift to Wolsey, but at dinner in the great hall tonight one of her ladies mentioned the episode, and Anne laughed. That was nothing, she said. It would cost her more than £20,000 in bribes before she had done with Wolsey. I saw Chapuys raise his head sharply and stare at her. He, as the Spanish ambassador, is of course on Catherine's side in all this. He will doubtless tell the Queen that Anne intends to bribe people so as to make sure Wolsey's downfall is complete, and Catherine will tell the Emperor Charles in the hope that he will make Henry see what a scheming minx Anne is. But Anne knows all that, and she does not care. She is certain now that she will soon hold all the power.

Oh why did the Pope not make a decision when this first started? The Holy Father's dithering has let the whole thing grow into a monstrous enmity between himself and King Henry. In order to get his own way, the King seems ready to flout the whole authority of the Catholic Church, and that must surely be the ultimate sin. Where will it all end?

4th March 1530

I did not want to come to Anne's household at Whitehall, for it meant another parting with my family, but Tom is here as well. He and I have seen each other every day, so these have been happy months. This place is not like Hever, though. There are no gardens, no meadows, no clear little river, only the grey width of the Thames, with all its boats and barges.

Rosanna is expecting a baby in the autumn. I shall be an aunt! Strangely, I found that I envied her. I never thought I would want marriage and children, being a restless girl who always wanted to be a boy – but in a way, I have had my wish. Anne regards me as her jester and entertainer, a singer and player who can dispel bad moods and bring amusement – but I had not imagined being in the service of a peevish, moody woman who wants nothing but to become Henry's queen. I grew up in the tempestuous warmth of Henry's court, with its masques and dances, its summer storms of fury and its gales of laughter, but this household is a tight-lipped one in which people have learned to be careful what they say.

Perhaps I am not by nature a court lady. Papa came from a family of troubadours, travelling from one country to another, with no expectation of becoming rich or powerful. When Mama first knew about Tom, she felt she had to remind me that a blacksmith would not bring me the advantages that would come through marrying an aristocratic husband – but she smiled as she said it, and I knew she was not very serious.

Tom and I share a dream that one day we will leave the King's service, if he will release us, and live in some small place of our own. Perhaps it will never be more than a dream, but we love thinking about it, planning what crops we will grow and where we will keep the pig and the cow, and whether we can afford a horse.

The dream may never come true, but at least it makes us happy. The King, on the other hand, looks increasingly irritable. During these winter months there have been some violent quarrels between him and Anne. She has always been sharp-tongued, and he admired her for that at first, liking her spirit, but there have been times when I have held my breath at some cheeky response of hers. After all, Henry is the king, and he commands respect, even from those he loves.

He repented of his severity to Wolsey, who has been ill throughout the winter, for at heart he has a great regard for his old friend and adviser. He sent him a formal pardon last week, though the Cardinal is still banned from any return to court. Anne was furious, naturally, and made some dark remarks to the effect that she had not finished with Wolsey yet. I think uneasily of her reference to the costs of bribery, and wonder what she is planning. Meanwhile, the Cardinal's health is improving a little. Perhaps the small sign of Henry's forgiveness has put new heart into him.

28th March 1530

Today has given me a personal cause to dislike the Boleyn family. Anne's brother George caught me by the waist and pulled me to him, causing me to spill wine down my skirt from the jug I was carrying. He turned my head with his strong hand and pressed a kiss on my mouth, asking why I chose to be so chaste and superior. I told him I was betrothed – though that is not strictly true – and tried to free myself from his grasp. He demanded to know who my chosen sweetheart was, but I would not tell him, for fear he would get Tom sent away. He released me at last, but not until I had endured much of his kissing and pawing of my body. I am a strong girl and had he been any ordinary man I would have used my fists and feet to send him packing, but he is Lord Rochford, much favoured by the King, and I dared not give him cause for complaint. Tom is furious.

20th July 1530

We hear that all the lords of England, Wolsey included, signed a petition to the Pope some weeks ago, asking him to decide in favour of dissolving the King's marriage. I was surprised to hear this of Wolsey, who has never liked Anne Boleyn, but I suppose he is anxious to keep in King Henry's favour. But it was no good, for his Holiness still refuses to consider a divorce. The Emperor naturally wants him to come down on the side of the Queen, and I suppose the Holy Father is in a quandary, not wishing to offend either of these powerful men. Henry has threatened to marry Anne whether he is still Catherine's husband or not.

7th August 1530

Wolsey has recovered from his illness now. Although he signed the petition to the Pope, there is a rumour about that he is in fact supporting Chapuys in his demands that Henry shall return to Catherine. When Anne heard of this, her lips narrowed to a tight line, and her black eyes were hard and determined. She said nothing, but I fear that Wolsey's effort to obey both his conscience and his king may have terrible results. Anne is determined, and she is utterly unforgiving.

22nd September 1530

Rosanna has had her baby! Mama's letter says it is a little boy, and he is well and strong, God be thanked. They are going to call him John. I think of Papa, who used to be known as Mr John by the English who could not get their tongues round Michel Valjean. He would have been so proud of his grandson. I cannot wait to see my little nephew, but wait I must, at least until Christmas, when I hope we will be together.

24th October 1530

My suspicions about Anne's intentions were dreadfully right. Cardinal Wolsey's physician has made a wild accusation about his master. He says Wolsey is secretly urging the Pope to excommunicate Henry and hand the rule of England over to Queen Catherine. We are all sure the man was bribed to tell such a story, and knowing glances are exchanged. Nobody has forgotten Anne's boast of how much she would spend to achieve Wolsey's downfall.

The King is deeply shocked. Can his old friend really be plotting against him? He paces about in scowling silence, unsure what to believe. Anne, of course, insists that the story is true. She sits beside him with her slim hand on his embroidered sleeve, whispering in his ear that Wolsey has planned this as a way to his own power, seeing himself as adviser to Catherine once Henry is deposed. "My lord," I heard her say, "you must protect yourself."

She looks impeccably concerned and serious, but I wonder what she is really thinking. Is it just a game to her, a sort of human chess where people may be deployed like pieces on a board, or does she understand that she is dealing with powerful and dangerous men? She obviously thinks she can persuade Henry to do whatever she wants, and at the moment this may be true – but it may not remain so. He adored Catherine for all the years of their happy marriage, and perhaps secretly still does, but he is ruthless in trying to rid himself of her now that his needs have changed. But Anne is a gambler, playing her game for the highest possible stakes. I sometimes wonder if she loves the danger more than she loves the King.

1st November 1530

My lady Anne has won. Today Henry drew up a warrant for the arrest of Cardinal Wolsey. By a strange irony, it will be carried out by Henry Percy, now the Earl of Northumberland, the young suitor who sought Anne's hand seven years ago and was dismissed by Wolsey. Truly, the lady's vengeance will be sweet to her. Percy has been chosen as the arresting officer, and I wonder if this was by her request. He leaves today for Cawood, in Yorkshire, to charge the Cardinal with high treason. And the punishment for that is death.

28th November 1530

Cardinal Wolsey will not have to face the humiliations of imprisonment and trial. He was a very sick man when Percy arrested him. One of the soldiers in the party said the Cardinal could hardly sit upright on his mule as they started on the long journey back to London. They had to keep stopping to do what they could to revive him, and by the time they reached Leicester it was obvious that he was dying. They sought refuge at the abbey there, and the monks tended Wolsey devotedly, but he died that night.

The King was grieved to hear the news. "I wish he had lived," he said.

What a strange man he is. How could he wish his old friend to have lived when he had just ordered his arrest and almost certain death on the scaffold? Henry always seems able to be two men at once, both the soft-hearted romantic and the ruthless despot.

Anne has no regrets, of course – quite the contrary. She laughed in triumph, and at once started planning an elaborate masque entitled *The Going to Hell of Cardinal Wolsey*. Many of us find the idea distasteful, but nobody dares say so.

21st December 1530

Once again we are at Greenwich for Christmas. I like this place so much better than Anne's palace at Whitehall. A grassy hill slopes down to the river, and Tom and I walk among the tall trees where the herons nest. Queen Catherine has joined us for Christmas, so my family is together again. It is lovely to see Mama, and the boys who both look so much bigger now. Daniel is twelve, a stocky boy, much more likeable than he was when we were children, and William has filled out and lost his paleness. I was especially delighted to see Rosanna and Diego and baby John. He is a beautiful child, with a mop of dark hair like the rest of us. I used to hold William when he was small, but I had forgotten how solid and how charged with life a baby feels. The little legs kick so strongly, and the fists wave in the air with excitement, ready to grab at a finger. Rosanna insisted on feeding him herself, though the other ladies were surprised. Most of them hand their children to a wet nurse. I would not want to do that. How does the baby ever know who his true mother is if another woman feeds him? But then children of the aristocracy have to get used to accepting things. They will have little choice about where they are sent or to whom they are married.

I thought it might be embarrassing for the Queen to be here with Henry and Anne, but the King treats his wife with great courtesy. He has her beside him at mealtimes and in the evenings to watch the masques and dancing. She looks pale and unwell, but she holds her head high, every inch the queen. It is good to have her here, in her rightful place. I do not have much chance to see her, as I have to wait on Madam Anne, who keeps mostly to her own chambers, but the warmth of Catherine's presence imbues the whole palace, and makes everyone feel more festive.

Christmas Day 1530

I shall remember this day for ever. As we walked across the frosty grass this morning, Tom asked me to marry him. He has been worried ever since Lord Rochford made his unwelcome approach to me. "If his lordship should set his mind on you instead of his shrewish wife, my objections would count for nothing," he said. "And if the King can divorce a wife he no longer wants, who is to say Rochford may not do likewise?"

We will have to ask the King's permission to marry. We both know he may not approve of one of Anne's ladies choosing a blacksmith as her husband, and I can only pray that he is in a good humour. I cannot imagine what we will do if he refuses.

27th December 1530

Tom and I were admitted to the King's presence this afternoon. I had hoped Queen Catherine would be with him, but she was not. We both knelt before him, and he listened to our request. Then he gave a bark of laughter. "Marry?" he said. "Aye, why not." He took a great draught from the cup of wine he held. "All the world seeks to marry." I could see that he was a little drunk, and felt glad of it, for wine usually improves his mood. Then he became more serious, and laid his hand first on Tom's head then mine. "Go with my blessing," he said. "Be married, by permission of your King."

I wept with gratitude and kissed his hand, and he laughed. "These are early days for tears," he said. "Those come later." His face clouded and he waved us away. "Go, leave me." And from loving him for his generosity, I once again found him alarming.

12th January 1531

We were married yesterday in the chapel here at Whitehall. The King was not present and neither was Anne, but Queen Catherine came, which gave me great joy. Mama was there, and my brothers, scrubbed and tidy and in their best clothes, and Rosanna and Diego and little John. All my friends in the court were there as well, and Chapuys came, perhaps because I am related to a previous Spanish ambassador. I only wished Papa could have lived to see this day. I almost wept as I thought of him standing at my side, and Tom understood. His hand tightened over mine, and I managed to smile. Papa would have liked

Tom – he always preferred the company of "practical men", as he called them.

There was a splendid dinner for us all afterwards. I was amazed, because I know I am not one of Anne's favourite ladies. One or two of them looked at me with a curl of the lip, but most of them were at least polite, if not downright admiring of my handsome husband. I heard someone whisper, "What a lovely couple they make!" And that is true. We are a couple, and we will love each other for ever.

Tom and I will have our own room now, in whatever house or palace my lady Anne occupies. We are man and wife. *Man and wife.* I say the words again and again. I am Elinor Freeman, a married woman.

21st January 1531

King Henry has a new adviser, Thomas Cromwell. He used to be in the service of Cardinal Wolsey, but he came to court some years ago and he has now replaced the Cardinal as the King's most favoured man. He has a heavy face and small eyes that remind me of a pig. There is a mean, shrewd look about him that frightens me. He was a mercenary soldier in Italy in his younger years, fighting on the side of whichever army paid him best, and I feel he is still capable of doing whatever he is asked to do, with no scruples. Coupled with the clever and calculating Thomas Cranmer, Henry now has formidable men on his side.

24th January 1531

We hear that the Pope has at last acted. He has sent a message to King Henry, commanding him to separate himself from Anne Boleyn and return to his lawful wife. It is too late. The King was not even angry. He just laughed.

7th February 1531

Today Henry went to Parliament and told them the Church in England would no longer answer to the rule of the Pope. Instead it would have the ruling monarch as its supreme head. I thought it was an outrageous proposal, and said English people would never accept it. Tom laughed. Nobody will object, he says. The monasteries and convents will be set against it, for without the backing of Rome they will lose much of their wealth and power – but why should ordinary people mind? Tom thinks they will like the idea that they can worship God and be aware of His divine will without the intercession of the priest. And he for one is all in favour of it.

Can Tom be right? I feel guilty for even thinking about it, as if God sees the doubt in my mind and may punish me. But the daffodils are starting to bloom and the birds sing in the lengthening days, and there is no sign yet of divine retribution. Perhaps it is true that the human soul can reach God without an appointed churchman to open the way. I can see why people might find the idea exciting. But no, I must not be tempted. In my heart of hearts, I know it is sinful.

11th February 1531

King Henry's proposal has been accepted. Archbishop Warham announced today that the Act separating the Church of England from Rome has been passed, "as far as the law of Christ allows". They say the Archbishop looked distressed as he made the announcement. Madam Anne is ecstatic, needless to say. Now that the rules have been rewritten, I suppose it is only a matter of time before Henry's divorce goes through and she becomes queen.

John Fisher, Bishop of Rochester, who defended the Queen at the Westminster hearing, says it is against God's law for a king to declare himself head of the Church. He is a brave man – and perhaps a foolish one. I was with Anne when she heard what he had said, and although she made no comment, her thin eyebrows rose over her black, beady eyes, and her lips set into their thin line of determination.

21st February 1531

I did not realize just what danger John Fisher was in. Yesterday everyone in his household collapsed at the table in terrible pain after eating the soup. Several of them are dead. Fisher himself had taken only a spoonful or two, but he was seized with agonizing stomach cramps. He is still very ill, as are the other survivors. The cook, Richard Rouse, has been arrested and accused of putting a poisonous white powder into the soup, but nobody believes the man did this of his own accord, if he did it at all. Quite clearly someone was bribed. And where did the poison come from? I hardly dare write the name. It is whispered that the powder was supplied by Lord Wiltshire. And he, of course, is Anne Boleyn's father.

We dare not guess whether the King was party to the plot to poison Fisher. He is determined to show his disapproval, so he has ordered a new punishment for poisoners. They are to be boiled alive. The unfortunate cook, Richard Rouse, is to suffer this terrible death.

8th March 1531

We are still at Greenwich, and the Queen remains part of the household, though there is constant gossip about when and how the royal divorce will take place. I think the King still hopes he may persuade Catherine to agree to a peaceful annulment of the marriage, for he goes to see her in her chambers from time to time, even though Anne throws a furious tantrum whenever he does. He looks aggrieved, and seems to be playing the part of a man forced by the need for an heir to separate from the wife he loves. And who knows, perhaps in some corner of his heart he does love Catherine still. At the same time, though, he is impatient to marry Anne.

Princess Mary is ill, and Catherine has begged the King to be allowed to go and see her in Wales. He said she could go by all means, but he added darkly, "and stay there". Mama heard the Queen's quiet answer. "I would not leave you for my daughter or for anyone else in the world." How steadfast she is, and how brave!

25th March 1531

The King relented. As Queen Catherine will not leave him, even for her daughter's sake, he sent for Princess Mary to come from Ludlow to London. Her procession arrived yesterday. She is very ill, but she survived the long journey and is now lodged at Richmond Palace. Henry allowed the Queen to join her there, and of course Mama went with her, for she will never be parted from Catherine. Rosanna and the others remain here.

19th April 1531

Mary's health is much improved now, and Catherine has come back to Greenwich, leaving her daughter in the care of Lady Salisbury.

A messenger from the Pope arrived a few days ago. He told the King his case can only be tried in Rome, and he may be excommunicated if he persists in making himself head of a separate English Church. Henry snorted with contempt. "I care not a fig for his excommunications!" he said.

4th May 1531

Queen Catherine asked Henry if Mary could come and join the court at Greenwich, but he was in one of his most irritable moods, and refused.

31st May 1531

A deputation of more than 30 peers and councillors went to see the Queen today and pleaded with her to give up her marriage. She sent them away, but not until she had told them the truth as she saw it. Mama heard what she said, and wrote it down while it was fresh in her mind. I am putting the words in this diary, because they are so brave:

> *I love and have loved my lord the King as much as any woman can love a man, but I would not have borne him company as his wife for one moment against the voice of my conscience. I am his true wife. Go to Rome and argue with others than a lone woman!*

Henry was bellowing with rage when the deputation came back to his quarters. He said he never wanted to see Catherine again. As far as he is concerned, the marriage is over. Although I love the Queen, and admire her courage, I begin to wish she could accept what has happened. If she would give in, things would be so much better for her. Out of gratitude if nothing else, Henry would be kind to her. As it is, she refuses to accept any judgement except that of the Pope, and she is turning herself into her husband's enemy.

We are shortly moving to Windsor, so once again I am busy packing.

23rd June 1531

The King was unexpectedly kind, and allowed Princess Mary to come with us, as well as Catherine. The stay at Windsor will only be a short one, however, as we are due to move to Woodstock on the 14th of next month. After that, I suppose we will set out on summer progress, for these great houses are grimy and stinking after the winter, and in great need of their summer cleaning.

14th July 1531

We were woken in the early dawn yesterday, and told to get ready at once, as we were leaving for Woodstock. It was hardly light, but we started to carry things down to the stable yard at the back of the palace, getting ready to start out. I could see no sign of Mama or Rosanna, but I assumed they were helping the Queen to get ready. I had not seen either of them for two or three days, as I had been so busy in Anne's quarters, sorting and packing clothes. Then Rosanna appeared, and stared in surprise at the horses and pack-mules being harnessed and the baggage being loaded. She was carrying little John because he had woken her for his early feed. She would not have heard us otherwise, for the Queen's household has its rooms on the far side of the castle, where the clatter and jingle of our preparations would not penetrate.

"I must tell Mama!" she said in alarm. "Nobody told us we were leaving so early."

The Duke of Suffolk heard her, and shook a warning finger. "Say nothing," he warned her. "Go back to bed."

She and I stared at each other, each of us understanding what the King had planned. Queen Catherine was to be left behind, without so much as a farewell. This was the final parting.

"Oh, Rosanna," I said, "when will I see you again?"

She shook her head. Neither of us knew.

We hugged each other.

"The poor queen," Rosanna whispered, and both of us wept.

A horn was blown and a man shouted the order to mount and move off. Tom waved from where he had been helping to hitch up the baggage carts, and called me to join him.

I so much wanted to run through the palace and at least say goodbye to Mama, but there was no time. Tom was on his horse now and clattering towards me, leading the bay mare I was to ride. I mounted, and turned in the saddle to touch Rosanna's hand for a last time, then we were moving across the yard and out into the lane. King Henry went past, spurring his black horse to the front of the line, and I saw that his face was set in grim determination.

I keep thinking of Queen Catherine waking to find everyone gone, with only her attendants left in that great, empty palace.

29th July 1531

I heard from Mama today for the first time since that dawn departure. She says the King sent a messenger to Catherine yesterday, telling her she must remove herself and her staff from Windsor. The Queen must have realized in that moment that Henry has truly left her, but even then, she kept her dignity. "Go where I may, I still remain his wife," she told the man, "and for him I will pray." She was grieved that he had left without saying goodbye, she added, and hoped he was well.

I understand now why there was such an outburst of fury from the King's chambers when the man came back from Windsor and went in to see him. We could hear Henry bellowing, "I want no more of her messages!"

He tries to brush her off, but she clings as cobwebs do to velvet, and the harder he brushes, the more closely she twines herself round his fingers.

6th October 1531

I am going to have a baby. It will be born in June of next year. I am so pleased. Tom is torn between joy and anxiety, but I tell him to have faith. Many women die in childbirth, it is true, but far more do not. Look at all the people who walk about on this earth, I told him. Each one of them has been born of some woman. And I am strong and healthy. I must admit, though, the days of being on summer progress were tiresome, as I often felt so sick and queasy. I have not told the Lady Anne my news. She is full of plans for her wedding, and has little interest in anything else. During any spare moments we have been busy cutting and stitching new clothes for her.

In the weeks of moving about there has been no news of Catherine, but I had a letter from Rosanna yesterday, saying that the Queen and her attendants are now at a place called Easthampstead. Princess Mary has been sent to Richmond. I suppose the King has realized he will never persuade Catherine to give him a divorce, but none of us can imagine what he will do about it now.

27th October 1531

Mama writes to say Catherine's court has now removed to The More, a manor house in Hertfordshire that was once owned by Cardinal Wolsey. It is a pleasant place, she says, well furnished and with fine parklands surrounding it. The Queen has been granted more servants, and at the end of this month, 30 Venetians are to visit her from Italy. Mama and her other ladies are frantically preparing for them, but I am glad they are seeing some life there. I was afraid the Queen was to be banished to a life of boredom and isolation. But then of course this visit will have been planned for a long time. Henry cannot have it said that he is failing in hospitality, and neither does he want people to say he is treating his royal wife badly.

We are busy at Ely Place in the City of London, preparing for a great banquet on 10th November, but Anne continually nags us to work harder at making her new clothes. I am sick of the sight of silks and velvets and tiny pearls to be stitched in intricate patterns on bodices and collars. She knows now that I am pregnant, but when I told her she merely said, "Are you, indeed." Other people's pregnancies annoy her, for she cannot wait to be the King's wife and give him the son he so desires. She must be at least 30 now, and sometimes she looks older, when her face sets into lines of bitterness and jealousy.

Tom overheard an alarming rumour today while he was shoeing the Duke of Suffolk's horse. (It is strange how the nobility will talk to each other in front of some menial person, as though they were not being heard and understood.) Anne has warned John Fisher not to attend the next session of Parliament, lest he should suffer a repeat of the stomach pains that almost killed him in February. Fisher refuses to support the King in his new control of the Church, and Thomas More agrees with him. More is one of Henry's oldest friends, but I wonder if even he is safe.

The King is in a constant state of fury these days. He is having trouble with an old injury to his leg, sustained during a joust some years ago. It has become infected and is very painful, so he has even less patience than usual. Last summer's progress annoyed him, for the people who stood along the roadsides were still shouting that they wanted to see Catherine, their rightful queen. He is angry with them, but he cannot force them to take Anne to their hearts. And, worst of all, the bishops and the parliament seem reluctant to take the final step of declaring the royal marriage null and void. Perhaps they are not sure how to do it. After all, such a thing has never happened before, in all the long history of England.

11th November 1531

The banquet at Ely Place was staged yesterday, for all the most important men in the City of London. I suppose this had been planned for a long time, before the King and Queen parted, but the occasion really was a very strange one. Since Henry now refuses to appear in public with his wife, he entertained half the guests in one hall and she the other half in another. The royal pair did not meet throughout the whole afternoon.

When Catherine left Ely Place to return to The More, a great crowd was standing outside to cheer her and shout their support, and this did not improve the King's temper. He is particularly furious at the moment because the Pope, after all these years of indecision, has summoned him to Rome for his case to be decided. One of the gentlemen ushers caught a glimpse of the papal document, and gleefully told us all of the words that caught his eye. They said Henry was to remove "that diabolic woman" from his bed and restore his rightful wife.

This makes everyone smile, for we all know that Anne, even yet, is not in the King's bed. With iron determination, she is waiting for marriage and the crown.

25th November 1531

A frightening thing happened last night. Anne Boleyn set out from here to dine with friends at a house by the Thames, being carried in a litter and accompanied by a small group of friends and servants, including myself. We had not gone far when a breathless man came running to warn us that a crowd was approaching – and sure enough, a multitude of women came pouring out of every street and converged on us, screaming abuse at Anne and trying to drag her from her litter. I was sure they meant to kill her and perhaps all of us. I was thrown into utter panic, not so much for Anne as for myself. In that awful moment, I could only think of the child growing inside me, and I was terrified that this small life might perish along with my own. Some of the creatures in the crowd, I could see, were men dressed as women, but they were all screaming that Anne must not be Henry's queen, and should be done away with.

Thanks to the warning, we were already heading fast for the river, and by great good fortune we were able to scramble aboard a barge and cast off with none of us harmed, but Anne was sobbing with panic, and all of us were very scared.

It is not only the common people who dislike Madam Boleyn. Her supporters at court are beginning to waver. She is so impatient with the King and speaks to him so impertinently that even her own uncles are embarrassed by her behaviour. She has upset the Dukes of Suffolk and Norfolk, and Sir Henry Guildford, who was Comptroller of the King's Household, has resigned his office and left the court, being deeply offended by something she said to him.

25th December 1531

For the first time ever, Henry has not invited the Queen to join us at court for Christmas, and the celebrations here seemed muted in her absence. Catherine sent him a gold cup, but he scowled when he received it, and gave orders that it should be returned. By contrast, he gave Anne a room hung with embroidered satin and cloth of gold. My lady, for all her tantrums, can still do no wrong.

Tomorrow she goes on a visit to her parents at Hever, and Tom and I have to be among those who go with her. It will only be a short visit, however.

8th January 1532

We are back at court in Greenwich. Anne has been installed in the chambers that used to be Catherine's. It is so strange to look round these familiar rooms, where I used to play and sing for that great lady, and tell stories to make her laugh. There is not much laughter here now, and what there is tends to be mocking or triumphant. It is seldom simply amused.

10th January 1532

Sir Thomas More has resigned from his office of Lord Chancellor. The whole court is agog that such an old friend of the King should desert him. Sir Thomas has never approved of Anne, and he was shocked to hear that Henry will not go to Rome for the Pope's judgement. Remembering what happened to Wolsey, I wondered if the King would order More's arrest, but he seemed saddened rather than angry. He is allowing his old friend to retire to his quiet house at Chelsea. At least for now.

25th January 1532

Henry has proclaimed that he is permitting Princess Mary to visit her mother at Enfield. He ordered this to be made widely known, and we can all see why. The people know now that Catherine spent Christmas on her own, and they mutter against the King for his bad treatment of his royal wife and daughter. For this reason, he is more than usually anxious to be seen as just and generous.

Today I felt the child inside me begin to move – just a small flutter, but I know it is alive and well. Anne Boleyn gives me more work to do than ever before, but the other women help me. I feel almost sorry for her. She is almost double my age, and she must be wondering if she will ever have a baby of her own.

23rd April 1532

King Henry is having increasing trouble with his subjects. On Easter Sunday, with the King and Anne before him in the church at Greenwich,

Friar William Peto had the incredible boldness (and courage) to preach against Anne Boleyn. He warned Henry that if he made an "unlawful" marriage with the woman who sat beside him, God would punish him as He had punished Ahab, and the dogs would lick his blood. The King turned purple with rage, and he walked out of the church with Anne hurrying at his heels. They say Peto is to be banished from the kingdom.

19th May 1532

Princess Mary's visit to her mother may well be her last, it seems. Mama writes from The More to say the Queen has been ordered to have no further contact with her daughter. Catherine has to leave The More and move to a place called Bishop's Hatfield, in Hertfordshire. She will miss Mary dreadfully. I am sure her loyal servants will carry messages between the two of them, but it is a sad thing all the same.

Meanwhile, the King is spending huge amounts of money on resplendent new clothes for Anne. Her requirements are far more than we can make here, so other dressmakers are at work. She has a gown of gold-embroidered velvet that cost £74, she boasts, and her latest order is for a black satin gown lined with black velvet, to be worn in her bedchamber if she chooses to receive guests there.

13th June 1532

The bishops are still deeply troubled at the idea of breaking away from Rome, and they understand very clearly that all this is happening because Henry wants to take a new wife. John Fisher preached against the union with Anne last week, and we all thought the King would be furious, but he shrugged it off. He has been much occupied, they say, in drawing up a new pact of friendship with France.

The whole thing is exhausting to think about. I often wish I could be in some other place, where life could be simple and straightforward. I am not often so tired and out of sorts, but the coming child makes me feel burdened and heavy.

2nd July 1532

Last week, on 26th June, my beautiful son was born. His name is Michael, after my father's French name of Michel, and he is strong and healthy. I am sorely exhausted, for the birth took a long time, but Tom cares for me well, and my friends among the court servants bring me small treats of beef and venison, with wine to build up my strength. How ironic it is that Tom and I have produced this boy child with no more than ordinary pain, while the King is tearing the country apart in his desperation to have a son.

28th August 1532

The summer progress did not last long this year. I was excused from going because my baby is so young, but Tom had to be with them, so I am selfishly glad the journeying was cut short. He says the crowds were so hostile to Anne that the King lost his temper and commanded a return to London. The servants are in a terrible panic because the cleaning is not finished.

The King's anger has reached out to touch Catherine, I suppose, because he hates the way she still has the people's support. A letter from Mama today says he has dismissed Maria de Salinas (now Lady Willoughby) from the Queen's service. It is a cruel thing to do, for Maria is Catherine's oldest friend. Mama, too, will miss her, for she was one of the original Spanish ladies, one of the few left in the Queen's household.

Old Archbishop Warham died last week. Henry does not bother

to pretend any regret, for Warham was one of Catherine's most loyal supporters. Thomas Cranmer will be the new Archbishop of Canterbury, and he, of course, is firmly on the side of the King. . .

30th August 1532

Someone left a book of prophecies in Anne Boleyn's apartments, and the lady found in it a crudely drawn picture of herself with her head cut off. I was with her when she opened the book. For a moment she stared at the picture as if in perplexity, but then she tossed it aside and said it was a mere bauble. She certainly has courage. I would have been terribly upset to find such a thing – and frightened, too.

The King is determined to suppress any hostility towards his chosen queen. A man called Thomas Abell was sent to the Tower last week for publicly criticizing Anne, and people say he is not the only one.

1st September 1532

Today, with much ceremony, King Henry made Anne Boleyn a peeress in her own right, here at Windsor. She is now the Marquess of Pembroke, a title never before given to a woman.

I listened carefully to the words the herald read out in the grand chamber as Anne knelt before the King. There was reference to the title being handed on to any child Anne might bear, but a glance ran round as it was said, and eyebrows were raised. I wondered why, and made a note to ask someone later.

Henry placed a gold coronet on Anne's head and draped the crimson velvet mantle of state about her shoulders, then raised her to her feet as the trumpets sounded.

Apparently the phrase about inheriting the title usually contains the words "*lawfully begotten* offspring". This time, these words had been omitted. To talk of offspring that are perhaps not lawfully begotten can only mean one thing. Madam Boleyn has at last allowed the King into her bed, and he knows she may be pregnant.

Since Michael was born, I have not been serving Anne in her chambers. She dismissed me impatiently when I came back, saying I would be more useful with a needle than with a chamber pot. I knew I irked her with my full bosom and my absences every few hours to go and feed my baby. I reminded her too sharply of the child Henry so desperately wants. So I have been stitching at her new regal clothes instead, and have only the words of the other ladies to tell me what has been happening. Or not happening.

If Henry is disappointed, he shows no sign of it. He seems full of good cheer, and takes an obvious delight in his royal mistress, constantly letting his hand rest over hers and exchanging a private smile with her. And of course he would look extremely foolish should he try to discard her now. After these years of turmoil on her behalf, he can hardly say he made a mistake.

There is soon to be a meeting with King Francis in France. A large royal party will be going, so we are thrown into the usual fever of preparation.

6th September 1532

An embarrassing difficulty has occurred. No French lady can be found who is willing to accept Anne Boleyn as a guest. Queen Eleanor refuses to do so, and so does the French king's sister, now Queen of Navarre, who has described Anne's behaviour as "the scandal of Christendom". I do not know what is to happen. Henry will not go without Anne, but he cannot take her unless proper arrangements can be made.

10th September 1532

Anne has demanded that Queen Catherine shall hand over her jewels so that she, Anne, may wear them during her visit to France. I know the Queen will refuse, for these are the jewels of state, for only a reigning queen to wear – but if Henry sends her a written order to comply with the request, she will have to obey.

Henry, meanwhile, obeys Anne. Because of her objections, he now hardly ever goes to see his daughter, Princess Mary, whom he loves. Last week, Anne threatened to bring Mary here to be one of her serving women. And then she added, with a laugh that chilled me, that she might give the princess "too much dinner". We all remember what happened at John Fisher's dinner table, and there can be no doubt what the lady meant. Mary is safer to stay away from this court.

6th October 1532

Tomorrow we depart for Dover, the King and Madam Anne, with a great train of attendants. My lady has insisted that I must accompany her, although she knows I do not want to leave my baby for a trip that will take several weeks. I cannot disobey, of course. Tom has to come as well. Little Michael is almost weaned, which is just as well, and the woman looking after him assures me he will be well cared for. I know this is true, but I am still wretched at the thought of going so far away and handing my son to somebody else. I never used to be afraid for myself, but I am full of terrors now. What if the ship sinks? What if I fall prey to some terrible foreign disease and never come back to see him again? But there is no help for it – I have to go.

No hostess was found for Anne Boleyn, so she and Henry will stay at the Exchequer Palace in Calais, which belongs to England. Anne will remain there while Henry goes on to meet with Francis in the French kingdom.

14th November 1532

I did not take my diary with me to France. There is much in it that I would not like Anne Boleyn's supporters to see, and on such a journey who could know whether personal things would be kept safe from prying eyes?

It took us three days to reach Dover. The Nun of Kent was waiting for us at Canterbury. Her worldly name is Elizabeth Barton, they tell me, and she has been prophesying doom for Anne and the King for years. She seemed a little mad, I thought. She began ranting against Anne, prophesying that King Henry would come to disaster if he went on keeping her company, and I was surprised that he did not have her arrested. Anne Boleyn's mother, the Countess of Wiltshire, suggested that Anne should make the Nun one of her serving women, thus forcing her to behave herself. Someone offered the post to the woman, but she turned it down with contempt and disgust, so I fear Elizabeth Barton has sealed her own fate. Thomas Cromwell, who was with us until we took ship, said he would deal with the matter, and his small, piggy eyes held a look of relish at the prospect.

We crossed to France in a ship called *The Swallow*. The voyage took seven hours, and I was wretchedly sick. I began to fear I would never see land again, so it was a great relief to me when we came to Calais. Various dignitaries met us there, and the inevitable welcoming speeches were made. Then they escorted us to the Exchequer Palace, and ushered Anne and the King to their communicating rooms.

There was feasting and merry-making for over a week, then on Friday morning Henry rode out of Calais to meet with the French king. He came back four days later, bringing King Francis and a great retinue to be entertained as his guests. Anne did not go down to greet them, and made no appearance during the following day. She stayed in her rooms for the whole of Saturday and most of Sunday, planning her grand entrance. During that time we were working hard, making masks and getting elegant clothes ready for Anne and ourselves.

We stayed upstairs on the Sunday night until the supper things had been cleared, then seven of us followed Anne down the great stairs. We looked very striking, I suppose, in our most gorgeous gowns and our jewelled and embroidered masks, and Anne herself was resplendent in cloth of gold slashed with crimson satin. Her sleeves were of silver cloth, bound with gold cords. With her slim figure and her dark hair laced with strings of seed pearls, I must admit, she looked magnificent. She walked boldly across to King Henry, extended her hand to him and asked him to dance, and the pair of them took the floor. The rest of us chose other gentlemen as our partners, and the revelry began. As the evening went on, King Henry pretended great surprise in taking off our masks and discovering who we were. For all his ferocity, he is still a boy when it comes to music and entertainment.

The French king left Calais two days later, but by then he had spoken several times with the Lady Anne, and seemed delighted with her. After he had gone, we stayed on for a fortnight longer, for no purpose but pleasure and amusement. I suppose Henry and his beloved were on a kind of honeymoon. We busied ourselves in packing all the things we could, ready for when calm weather should return. For days on end, the sea was impossibly rough.

On Tuesday 11th November, we heard that the wind was set fair for England, so we sailed to Dover. This time, the crossing was easier, and my queasy stomach was soothed by the knowledge that Tom and I would soon be with our little son again. And, thank the Lord, he seems no worse for the parting.

Christmas 1532

Rumour has it that Anne Boleyn is pregnant. We wait to hear whether this is true.

9th January 1533

Anne Boleyn is indeed expecting a child. We are all in a flutter of excitement, wondering what the King will do now. He is still married to Queen Catherine, but he will be desperate to marry Anne and legitimize the coming heir – they say he is sure the baby will be a boy. Can he really take a second wife? It seems utterly illegal to me, but perhaps King Henry can make his own laws now.

25th January 1533

I woke before dawn this morning because Michael was crying. I picked him up and stood rubbing his back to ease him – and I could hear that people were moving about somewhere in the royal chambers. There was the thud of a muffled door and the murmur of voices, and after a little while an incantation of Latin began, with responses from a man's voice and then a woman's. My spine prickled in the darkness, for I was sure I was hearing a marriage service. The King's private chapel opens from his own quarters below our room in this palace of Whitehall.

When the baby quietened, I tucked him back into his cradle and crept back to cuddle in beside Tom. He was awake, too, and we murmured together, sharing our suspicion that Anne Boleyn was becoming a second wife to the King.

It was morning when we woke again. We set about the work of the day, and nothing was said by anyone of what had happened before dawn – and yet I caught a glance exchanged between Lady Berkeley and Anne Savage which made me certain they shared a secret knowledge. If there was indeed a marriage ceremony, Anne Boleyn would be attended by at least two ladies – and these two would be the most likely, being her favourites. No doubt we will hear the truth when it suits the King to announce it.

5th February 1533

Anne Boleyn cannot resist boasting about her pregnancy, though it is still supposed to be a secret. In front of a large group of courtiers, she told Thomas Wyatt, the poet, she had an insatiable craving for apples. The King had told her this was a sign of pregnancy, she added, but of course it could be no such thing. And she laughed. Thomas Wyatt was once in love with Anne himself, but those days are long gone. He looked embarrassed by what she said. One of the serving men overheard him telling Chapuys that he felt ashamed of her, I suppose to make it clear that he no longer has any liking for Anne. Chapuys will no doubt pass this on to the Queen, whom he devotedly supports.

18th February 1533

A letter from Mama brought bad news today. The King has ordered Queen Catherine to move her small household to Ampthill, a house she has visited many times as a royal wife and head of the court. Now she will be sent there with no company but her few attendants, and the place is quite far from London. Mama says the poor lady feels she has been banished, and this seems very true. She spent a wretched Christmas alone, and she is far from well.

I am sure King Henry piles on these hardships in the hope that Catherine will give in and agree to an annulment of her marriage. Had she done this when he first asked, he would most probably have treated her well and continued to visit her. In fact, at times when Madam Boleyn was being temperamental and impatient, Henry might have been glad to return to the arms of a loving and ever-tolerant wife.

But Catherine is the daughter of a warrior queen, Isabella of Spain, and her pride will never allow her to give in. She has told Mama many times that she would rather die than have her marriage to Henry considered illegal.

25th February 1533

There was a great banquet here last night. The King was behaving like a young bridegroom, kissing Anne before the whole company, and carousing with his friends. As the evening went on, he became very drunk. He was roaring with laughter and pouring out incoherent words, but we all grasped what he meant when he swept an arm round the great hall with its sumptuous hangings and its tables resplendent with gold plate, and said what a rich marriage his sweetheart had made. *Had made.* Eyebrows were raised as those who were still sober glanced at each other. The secret is out now. Henry and Anne are indeed married. The King has two wives.

8th April 1533

Anne's brother, Viscount Rochford, has been away for three weeks in France, on a secret mission. We all guessed that he went to tell the French king of Henry's marriage and Anne's pregnancy, and I think we were probably right. Rochford returned yesterday, and was closeted with Henry for a long time – and today the King made the official announcement that he has married Anne Boleyn and that she carries the royal heir. He appointed the Dukes of Norfolk and Suffolk to break the news to Queen Catherine, and they have already left for Ampthill.

11th April 1533, Good Friday

Archbishop Cranmer has asked the King for formal permission to judge on the question of annulling his marriage to Catherine. I cannot see by what authority the Archbishop can take it on himself to give a ruling – but I suppose everything is different, now the King no longer respects the word of the Pope.

13th April 1533, Easter Sunday

Yesterday, Anne Boleyn went in grand procession with King Henry to hear Mass. She was sumptuously gowned and decked with the jewels, and 60 of us accompanied her, all dressed in our silks and velvets. The whole court was uneasy at this parading of her before the public as Henry's new queen. How can she truly be queen when Henry is still married to Catherine? There is a terrible shamelessness about it. Anne's slender body shows the thickness of her pregnancy very clearly, and she glories in it. The people stared at her in silence as she passed, then muttered among themselves.

The King was obviously nettled by this continued public dislike. On return from Mass, he demanded that we all respect his lady as Queen of England, and says she will be crowned on Whit Sunday, 1st June.

This evening he read out the names of those who will form part of Anne's royal household. Her uncle, Sir James Boleyn, will be chancellor, and another relative, William Cosyn, her Master of Horse. I am to be among her ladies, and so is Anne Saville. Others include the Lady's cousin, Madge Shelton, Anne Gainsford, Lady Berkeley, Jane Seymour and Elizabeth Holland, who is the mistress of another of Anne's uncles, the Duke of Norfolk.

I quake inwardly to think of what would happen should Henry's new queen guess how much I detest the idea of this new arrangement. I have never fawned upon her as some of the other ladies do, and wonder sometimes why she seems to like me. I can only suppose it is because I play and sing well, and can keep her amused. Or perhaps she enjoys the fact that I have to serve her, whether I like it or not.

15th April 1533

I had a letter from Mama today. She was much distressed by the visit of the Dukes of Norfolk and Suffolk last week. They told Catherine she was no longer queen, merely the Princess Dowager of Wales. Henry has agreed that she may keep her property – what remains of it – but he will not pay her servants' wages or meet her household expenses after Easter.

The King's harshness appals me, but I suppose he cannot believe that his own wife continues to defy him. She does so out of love, because she has devoted her life to him, but her love has become an iron cage to her husband now, and he would do anything to break it. How terrible that a marriage should wither away to such a bitter ghost of itself.

I heard today that a woman called Margaret Chancellor has been thrown into prison for referring to Anne as "a goggle-eyed whore".

She is not the only one to say such things, though the wise take care to speak only among trusted friends.

23rd May 1533

On the 10th of this month, Cranmer brought a court of judgement together to give a final verdict on the King's case, and today the judges declared King Henry's marriage to Catherine of Aragon null and void.

So it is done at last. I knew it had to happen, but I am filled with a deep sadness. Princess Mary, we hear, faced the assembled clerics bravely, telling them she would never accept that her mother was anything other than the rightful Queen of England. Catherine herself never appeared before the court.

28th May 1533

This morning Archbishop Cranmer announced from a high gallery in Lambeth Palace that he found the King's marriage to Anne "good and valid". It was like a signal for the celebrations to start, for within a few hours Anne was on her way up the river from Greenwich to the Tower, where she will stay as custom demands until she is crowned Queen of England this coming Sunday. What a wonderful sight it was! The Lord Mayor of London and all his aldermen escorted her up the river in a multitude of boats and barges, all sumptuously equipped with awnings of cloth of gold. Banners and streamers fluttered, and the air was full of music, for bands of musicians had been crammed on to the decks of barges and played constantly. I was glad not to be among them, for it was far more fun simply to be among the ladies escorting Anne. Poor Mark Smeaton confessed to me yesterday that he was terrified he might be pushed into the water, playing in such a crowd, but I laughed and patted his shoulder. Mark is always afraid the worst will happen.

Anne sat enthroned in the royal barge, wearing a gown of silver-white tissue, and with her dark hair loose and flowing. She is visibly pregnant, of course, being six months gone, but she looked bridal all the same, and made a fitting centrepiece to the great pageant. So many boats surrounded us that they filled the river from bank to bank, all resplendent with their coloured awnings and with pennants flying. It was as if a host of brilliant butterflies had settled on the water with folded wings of purple and crimson, scarlet and silver and gold.

When we came to the Tower, there was a salvo of welcoming gunfire from the cannon that pointed their long barrels across the river, and the noise was so shattering that I clapped my hands over my ears, as did most people. Tom tells me additional guns had been brought in, so there were more than a thousand. Their combined thunder shook the air so violently that every pane of glass in the Tower and in the neighbouring buildings was broken.

The King was waiting for Anne, and as she stepped ashore at the entry to the Tower he kissed her fondly. Then he led her into the royal apartments, which have been freshly decorated and refurbished. He will stay with her there for two nights, then on Saturday he will go ahead of her to Westminster Hall, ready to receive her when she arrives in grand procession for a civic reception. The coronation itself will be on the following day.

Anne's uncle, the Duke of Norfolk, organized all these celebrations. He has done a wonderful job, being the efficient man he is, but I have seen a glance of tight-lipped disapproval on his face in recent days when he looked at his niece. People say he has not forgiven her for so shamelessly flaunting herself as the King's mistress. All the same, the Boleyn tribe must be pleased that they now hold such power in the court. Anne is able to confer immense benefits on those whom she favours. Norfolk himself has cause to be indebted to her, for his daughter married the King's natural son, Henry Fitzroy, and Anne even ensured that no dowry was demanded.

31st May 1533

Anne left the Tower this morning and was taken with great ceremony through London to meet the King at Westminster Hall. There was no lack of brilliance in the procession – it extended half a mile behind her, they say, and we were all magnificently dressed and mounted on fine horses – but the people were oddly reluctant to celebrate. It seemed they came merely to stare.

They had glorious things to stare at. Anne was carried in a litter hung with white cloth of gold, drawn by two white palfreys, and she wore her hair loose under a gold circlet studded with jewels. To shelter her, riders on either side of her carried a canopy on gold poles hung with small silver bells. The tinkling of these bells could be heard with embarrassing clarity in the silence, for the crowds lining the streets did not cheer. They should have been roistering and happy, for the public fountains ran with wine, but they remained obstinately unfestive. Few of the men even bothered to remove their caps in respect, and there was hardly a cheer.

Some of the courtiers in our procession shouted abuse at the people, berating them for their discourtesy – but then a worse thing happened. Some wit in the crowd pointed to the intertwined initials,

H and A, that appeared on every banner, and shouted ironically, "HA! HA!" In the next moment dozens of other voices had taken it up, and jeering laughter rang through the London streets.

Anne was distressed and angry by the time we reached the hall in Westminster for her state reception, and I am not surprised. She has waited and worked many years for this day, and the moment of her triumph has turned sour. I have never liked her, and I disapprove of much that she has done, but today I could not help feeling sorry for her.

Sunday 1st June 1533, Coronation Day

A great train of us walked from the Hall to Westminster on this Whitsunday morning. Anne wore a purple velvet cloak over a gown of crimson velvet edged with ermine, and her hair was again flowing loose, beaded with pearls and caught by a golden coronet. Red carpeting covered our way and stretched right through the Abbey to the high altar.

Again the crowds stood in silence, few men even bothering to take off their caps. The women eyed the pregnant queen with dislike, knowing Anne and Henry were not married when the child was conceived. No common woman could parade herself through the streets in such a condition, and they do not see why "the King's whore", as she has so long been called, should now be honoured. I saw the Nun of Kent, ranting as usual on a street corner and waving her fist, and they tell me she was arrested later. I am only surprised that pig-faced Cromwell waited so long.

When it was all over, I heard Chapuys say the coronation was "a cold, meagre and uncomfortable thing", but I feel he was being a little ungenerous. The people were cold, certainly, but within Westminster Hall the banquet that followed the coronation ceremony was magnificent. Course followed course, trumpeters played, and the music and celebration was glorious. It was something of a trial for Anne herself. She sat on a high dais in full view of the revellers, but her pregnancy is putting pressure on her bladder and she needs to relieve herself frequently. Two women were hidden beneath the sumptuous cloth, and when the need arose, they lifted the Queen's skirts for her and provided a receptacle. I would not have been in their place for anything.

There are days of merriment to follow, with jousting and hunting and dancing. I will enjoy it, for with so many musicians here, my services will not be so much in demand. As a court lady attending Anne, my main duty will be to join wholeheartedly in the revels – and who could be so mean-minded as to resent such a pleasant task? I feel almost guilty, though, for Tom is not here to share in all this celebration. He is a blacksmith, not a courtier, and throughout these days he has been at home with Michael. It was not my choice to be here, and if Tom and I follow our dream of living in some small place of our own, this may be the last grand occasion I will see. "Enjoy it, my sweetheart," Tom said. "Such a thing is something to remember. You will tell your grandchildren about it." And he is right, of course.

28th June 1533

To my joy, I find I am pregnant again. Michael was a year old two days ago, and it will be good for him to have a little brother or sister. I have written to tell Mama. She is starting to pack up the Queen's belongings, for in a month's time they have to transfer to a small and reputedly damp house at Buckden, in Huntingdonshire.

Anne is of a great size now, and constantly complains that the coming baby has ruined her figure. I think she mentions this so often in order to remind everyone that she carries the King's hoped-for son.

Chapuys has been saying he fears Henry may have Catherine murdered, and perhaps Mary as well, so exasperated is he with his ex-wife's obstinacy. When given an official notice of the court's judgement on her marriage, Catherine scored out the words "Princess Dowager" that had been used to describe herself. She insists that she is still the Queen.

I think the Spanish ambassador overstates his fears. The King is so taken up with Anne and the coming child that he hardly thinks of anything else. He has made no plans to go on progress this year. We are preparing to remove Anne's household to Hampton Court, where she will rest through the summer weeks, and Henry will stay near London so he can see her when he wishes. After some weeks at Windsor, we will go to Greenwich for the actual birth.

The Nun of Kent was brought before Archbishop Cranmer a few days ago, and he released her with the warning that she must stop ranting in the streets and inciting the people. She has been lucky.

11th August 1533

Mama writes to say they have now removed to Buckden. It is in the Fen country, wild and desolate, and the house is surrounded by a moat, which increases its dampness as well as making the Queen feel cut off from the outside world. People ran beside her procession as she came to the place, calling good wishes to her and saying they would serve her and, if necessary, die for her.

Catherine has little money now, Mama says, and food is sparse, but even so the Queen often fasts throughout the day, eating nothing. She gives what coins she can spare to the poor people of the parish, and next to her skin, Mama says, she wears the hair shirt of the Order of St Francis to remind her of the dangers of arrogance and self-indulgence.

She still works at her beautiful embroidery, producing altar-cloths for the churches in the district, but many hours of each day pass in prayer.

Anne has demanded that Catherine send her the christening gown that was brought from Spain. I was outraged to hear of this, for the gown is Catherine's personal property, worn by the infant Mary for her christening. Mama worked on its embroidery, together with the Queen herself. The Lady goes too far here – she cannot make Catherine give it up.

Mama's letter says the Pope has drawn up the papers to excommunicate Henry for his illegal marriage to Anne – but Catherine has begged His Holiness not to deliver them to the King. In her eyes, to be cut off from the Church and unable to share in its direct connection with God is the most terrible thing that can happen to the human soul, and she cannot bear this to happen to her husband, even though he has deliberately courted it.

18th August 1533

What a scene there was today! Anne has found out that her royal husband has been having an affair with some other lady. I don't know who it is, for we came here to Greenwich Palace just a few days ago to await the birth of the baby, and the court gossip has not reached me.

It reached Madam Boleyn, however, and she is furious. She screamed at Henry and called him names, and he was equally angry. He expects his wife to settle down into the background of his life now, bearing children and putting up uncomplainingly with whatever he chooses to do.

He berated Anne, undeterred by the fact that Jane Seymour and I were in the room. He regretted giving her a magnificent French bed, he told her, and had it not just been delivered, he would have stopped the order. She must remember that she had been made queen purely by his favour, and he could humble her again whenever he chose. With that, he walked out of the room and did not come back.

I would have been in tears at such a scolding, but Anne tossed her head, and her lips were pressed tight. She seems not to realize that her trump card has been played now, and she has no more bargaining power. She has given the King what he wants, in the form of the child that waits to be born, and there is no more thrill of the chase. He will turn for his amusement to other young women now, not as potential wives but in the same spirit that he will follow a deer or a wild boar through the forest. King Henry is above all a hunter. Catherine understood this, and waited with dignity for her husband to return to her from his latest chase, which he always did until Anne refused to be caught. Henry expects Anne to do the same, but she has not realized that this is a duty of the royal wife.

That is the trouble, I suppose, with a girl who has not been brought up in aristocratic circles. For all her love of power, Anne has common instincts, much as I do. She wants a husband who truly loves her and will be faithful to her. But Anne's husband is not like my Tom. He is a king. Women are a delight to him and he loves them quite sincerely for a while, but they are part of the great game of power, and will be discarded as soon as he tires of them.

27th August 1533

The Nun of Kent has been prophesying again, despite her warning from Cranmer a month ago, and it seems she is a complete fraud! She admits now that she has never had a vision in her life. I cannot imagine they will release her this time.

29th August 1533

Anne has insisted that Princess Mary be brought here, to work in her service. It's an outrageous order. Mary is a royal princess and heir to the throne. To make her attend during the birth of the half-brother who is meant to take her place as heir is an act of pure spite, but we all understand its purpose. This will be Anne Boleyn's sweetest moment of triumph. I never thought Henry would agree to such a suggestion, but he has not forgiven Mary for defending her mother so vigorously when the divorce was announced. Anyone who stands up for Catherine now incurs his fury. Even his own daughter.

7th September 1533

Anne's labour began early this morning, and at three in the afternoon she was delivered of a healthy child – but it is a girl. If there is any triumph, it must be Princess Mary's, who now remains first in line to be the Queen of England.

The King is bitterly disappointed. He barely glanced at his new daughter, though she is a lovely baby with red-gold hair like his own. Her name will be Elizabeth.

10th September 1533

Anne is a devoted mother. She adores her baby girl, seeming unperturbed by Henry's displeasure, and wants to feed the child herself. This will not be allowed, of course. A queen does not suckle her children like a cow suckling a calf. A common woman has already been engaged as a wet nurse, and Anne will have to be content with holding her daughter at the times permitted by the pattern of the royal day. Poor thing – I would hate such interference.

The Nun of Kent has been sent to the Tower. And Bishop Fisher is under house arrest. I have not heard what the charge against him is to be, but Anne has been complaining about him ceaselessly ever since he survived the poisoned soup.

2nd October 1533

The King did not attend his daughter's christening. I hear the official announcement of the child's birth now bears a clumsy amendment because there was no space left in which to change the word, "Prince" to "Princess". This made me laugh, but Anne of course does not find it amusing. She knows I am pregnant again, and yesterday she looked at me and said, "I will not be far behind you." She has failed to produce a son this time, but at least she has survived the birth, and little Elizabeth is strong and healthy. All she can hope for is to produce another child as soon as possible, and that it will be male. Meanwhile, Henry has again been unfaithful to her, and again, Anne made a fuss. She does not learn.

4th December 1533

Anne expects a second child, she announces.

Henry has now sent little Elizabeth away to Hatfield Palace, where, at three months old, she will have her own staff and household. To be fair to him, Hatfield is a healthier place than London, with its smoke-filled and noxious air, but Anne will miss her little daughter. I feel sorry for her.

Princess Mary is to go to Hatfield as an attendant to her little half-sister. In fact, she loves the baby and cares for her devotedly, but we all know the intention is further to humiliate her. Ever since Elizabeth's birth, Anne's malice against the daughter of Queen Catherine – or the Dowager Princess, as she is now supposed to be known – has become positively savage. Mary has been stripped of her title of Princess, and is effectively reduced to being a servant. Her household at Beaulieu is to be disbanded, and Henry is giving her manor house to Anne's brother.

10th December 1533

Henry decided to visit his little Elizabeth in Hatfield, and set out without saying anything to Anne about it. What a rumpus it caused! When the Lady found out where he had gone, she flew into a rage, convinced that his real purpose was to see Mary and perhaps make his peace with her.

Anne sent for Cromwell and commanded him to set out after the King to make sure he had no contact with Mary. Pig-face evidently did his job well, for the King's elder daughter was not to be found during the royal visit. On departing though, Henry glanced back, and saw her on a balcony. She fell on her knees to him, entreating him to stay. For a moment, the King hesitated as if inclined to turn back, regardless of Anne's wrath. He swept off his hat and bowed to Mary, and all the courtiers did likewise. But then he rode away.

We have heard since that Anne has demanded possession of all Mary's jewellery, saying that his "bastard daughter" has no right to it.

14th December 1533

Catherine has asked if she may be transferred to somewhere less damp and cold, as her health is suffering. Anne cruelly suggested she should go to Somersham, which everyone knows to be even worse than the Huntingdonshire house. Chapuys protested to Henry that this was impossible, and apparently the King smiled benignly and said she could go to Fotheringhay. Chapuys thinks he has scored a victory, but we all know Fotheringhay is even worse than Somersham, so he has done the poor lady no service. However, Henry has given his instructions, and the Duke of Suffolk is to be sent with a detachment of the King's Guards to force Catherine to obey the order.

The Duke does not want to go. He married a young bride only three months ago, and to ride to a cold and uncivilized county in December is not at all to his liking. He told Maria de Salinas, we hear, that he hoped he and his troops would meet with some mishap on the way that would force them to return, and I am sure his soldiers agree with him.

22nd December 1533

The Duke is having a difficult time of it in Huntingdonshire. Tom spoke to the man who rode from there yesterday with a message for the King, and heard the full story. On hearing that she was to move to Fotheringhay, Catherine locked herself in her room and said he would have to break the door down if he wanted to get her out.

The Duke could not do this, obviously. After all, Catherine belongs to the most powerful royal family in Europe. Her nephew is Charles of the Habsburgs, a warlike and domineering emperor who is quite capable of attacking any country whose ruler displeases him. We all know Henry would have been much firmer in dealing with his ex-wife, had it not been for the lurking fear that complaints from her to Charles might turn the Emperor against the English king. Mama has always said the Queen would not dream of stirring up trouble for Henry, as she adores him, but perhaps men who think only in terms of politics and power do not realize that.

Anyway, the Duke dismissed almost every member of Catherine's staff, leaving only the Spanish ones, and arrested her two chaplains for refusing to call her the Dowager Princess. The dismissed servants told the local people what was going on, and within a short time the village men were standing silently along the moat that surrounds Buckden, armed with cudgels, pitchforks and whatever other weapons came to hand.

Suffolk will not be having a very happy Christmas. And neither will I, for I worry about Mama. It will not be so bad for Rosanna, for she has Diego to help and support her. Mama, though, is deeply devoted to the Queen, and she will be so anxious and fearful. And what of my brothers? Daniel is fifteen now, and has been working in the Queen's household for quite some time. William has been making himself useful as well, since he is twelve, but neither of them has learned to speak good Spanish. Will they have been sent away? I can only wait to find out.

I hate this dark time of the year, when the days are so short and the nights so long and cold. Tom says we must look forward to the spring, when our next baby will be born – but it seems a long time away.

26th December 1533

In the middle of the feasting and merry-making, I cannot help thinking of my family and Queen Catherine, prisoners in that cold, damp house. The Duke of Suffolk and his men are still there, though none of us can see why. Perhaps they are making sure the dismissed servants do not sneak back into the building and continue to serve the Queen.

The last rider who came back said the villagers are still surrounding the house, for they love their queen, and will die in her defence if necessary. No letters have come from Rosanna or Mama. Tom says I must trust in God, for there is nothing I can do, and he is right, of course. But it is hard not to worry.

Anne's Christmas present to Henry was a great basin made entirely of gold and set with rubies and pearls. It contains a diamond-studded fountain in the form of three naked nymphs, whose nipples spout jets of water. There were cries of admiration, of course, but afterwards I heard one lady whisper to another, "My dear, did you ever see anything so vulgar?"

6th January 1534

Suffolk and his men are back from Buckden, the King having ordered their return, and my brothers are with them, thank the Lord. William has a bad cough and looks very thin and white, but Daniel is his usual robust self. The Queen has set him to work in the stables, where Tom is keeping an eye on him. He is going to teach him to shoe horses, and that will be good, for a man with a skilled trade can always earn a living. I gave William some chicken broth and put him to bed in our room, but he shivers in spite of the blankets.

The soldiers are grumbling and cursing at having spent a cold and miserable Christmas under the gaze of hostile villagers, and one of them who saw Catherine was horrified by how old and frail she looked. Suffolk himself told the King his ex-wife seems to be suffering from some serious illness, but if Henry was moved by this news, he did not show it.

The letter that one of the soldiers brought me from Mama said the house had been stripped of almost all its furniture, and the place is terribly bare and cold. The Queen's few remaining servants are all Spaniards, or at least part-Spaniards like Rosanna, and every one of them pretended to speak no English when questioned. The Bishop of Llandaff speaks Spanish, and he has been permitted to stay as Catherine's chaplain. But these things seem a scant comfort.

17th January 1534

William seems better. He ate some stewed venison today, then slept again. Daniel is very happy, working with Tom. I found him in the forge this morning, hammering a piece of red-hot iron and making the sparks fly. I wrote to Mama today to tell her the boys are both safe, and gave the letter to a rider who was carrying messages to her chaplain.

Someone has given Henry a peacock and a pelican. They are wonderful birds to look at, but they make a terrible noise, especially the peacock. Anne has complained that they disturb her sleep, so they are to be handed on to Sir Henry Norris in Greenwich. I have always liked Norris – he seems one of the nicest and most obliging of Henry's gentlemen. I hope he and his wife sleep more soundly than Lady Anne does.

23rd February 1534

Outbreaks of rebellious talk about Anne crop up everywhere. I have heard reports of people saying that Henry is living with his new queen in adultery, and Henry Percy, who once loved Anne, said openly the other day that she was "a bad woman". The King is seething with anger.

Lord Dacre has been tried for treason. We all feared for him, as he has been outspoken in his defence of Catherine, and has constantly opposed Anne. But after he had spoken for seven hours in his own defence, the jury unanimously acquitted him. This has not improved the King's temper.

William is recovered enough to start working as a kitchen boy.

He has been turning the spit today, and his face was pink from the heat of the fire and the smell of the roasting meat clung to him.

23rd March 1534

Today Parliament passed the Act of Succession. It means that any subject who says or writes anything derogatory about the King and his new wife will be guilty of high treason, for which the penalty is death.

I find this very frightening. As my father's daughter I grew up in the happy assumption that all things were open to be laughed at, even if one had to be cautious about the moment chosen for the joke. Surely it is the right of all English people to hold their own opinions, and to shout them in the street if they choose? I am sad to think that King Henry, whose roar of laughter has gladdened the court as often as his rages have silenced it, has lost all humour. Our great, outrageous, theatrical monarch is turning before our eyes into a tight-mouthed tyrant.

25th March 1534

Under the new Act, all citizens have to swear an oath of allegiance to Henry as Supreme Head of the State and of the Church. Nobody in the court refused, naturally, though there are many who obeyed only out of fear. I count myself among these, but with my new baby due to be born any day now, how can I do otherwise? I have not been to Mass for a long time, but if God can really listen to an ordinary woman who speaks only for herself, I hope He will understand that I have to work in the Queen's service and also to care for my little boy and my husband. I get very tired sometimes. It is no excuse, I know, for neglecting my religion. I do think about it, but I am not the stuff of which martyrs are made.

There are some who are. Thomas Abell, who was for a long time Catherine's chaplain, has been accused of treason because he steadfastly refuses to take the oath. Both he and John Fisher, no longer recognized as a bishop, have been imprisoned in the Tower, pending trial.

I find myself full of despair tonight. We seem surrounded by cruelty, and my strength fails me.

1st April 1534

My feeling of sudden weakness gave way that same night to the first pains of birth. It was a long labour, but by four the next afternoon my little daughter was born. She is a fine, big child, and Tom adores her. I would have liked to call her Catherine, but it is too dangerous, so she is to be Maria, after the ex-Queen's close friend, Maria de Salinas.

It was a long and difficult birth, and for two days I was very ill, but my strength is starting to return now. William comes up from the kitchen as often as he can, bringing me bowls of soup and small slices of lean meat. He is such a kind boy.

11th April 1534

A letter came from Mama today, and I had to laugh when I heard her news. The Pope, years too late, has judged King Henry's new marriage to be illegal. He has commanded the King to take Catherine back, and to pay the whole costs of the case, which must by now be astronomical. His Holiness might as well try to put a thunderstorm into a cooking pot.

Tom tells me Sir Thomas More has for the second time refused to take the oath of allegiance. He resigned from office two years ago, and since then Henry has constantly tried to win his approval for the new religion, but with no success.

17th April 1534

Sir Thomas More was sent to the Tower today. He is imprisoned in the Bell Tower, just above the cell where John Fisher is still being held. So much for old friendship.

Henry and Anne have been to Eltham Palace to visit little Elizabeth and to inspect the nursery that is being prepared for "the coming prince", as they confidently call their expected baby. They seem to have great faith in the power of their own wishing. I suppose it is natural to them, when everything else they can dream of is theirs to command. But the womb is mysterious, and its workings are known only to the will of God.

20th April 1534

Today the Nun of Kent and four others convicted of high treason paid a dreadful price for their crimes. They were taken from their cells in the Tower to a gibbet, where they were hanged, but not mercifully. Before they were dead, they were cut down and then beheaded.

13th May 1534

The Queen's small household has now been sent to Kimbolton Castle in Huntingdonshire. The rider who came from there today says it is a pleasant place, but Catherine has been allocated only two rooms. To my great joy he brought letters from Mama and Rosanna. Rosanna says the Bishop of Durham came the other day and tried to make Catherine take the oath. He even reminded her of the death penalty for refusing, but although she is very ill now, with terrible pains in her chest, she continued to refuse.

The Queen taught her servants well. Those who claimed to speak no English were allowed to take the oath in Spanish, and they said, "*El Rey se ha heco cabeza de la Iglesia*," which means, "The King has made himself head of the Church," and is no oath at all. What spirit Catherine has!

28th June 1534

A disaster has occurred, but it is being hushed up. Anne has lost the baby she was expecting. Nobody knows if the child was still-born or died shortly after the birth. We do not even know whether it was a boy or a girl, if it was christened or where it is buried. I am haunted by the knowledge that this small soul was so unlovingly disposed of after its few minutes in this world.

The whole thing is a mystery. Anne was nearly eight months pregnant, so the baby should have had a good chance of survival. None of the ladies known to me attended the birth, only the King's physician. Anne is up and about again now, seeming no worse for the experience except that her face is white and anxious, but Henry is grim with disappointment. Certainly he is fast losing faith in the wife who has cost him so much trouble and made him so unpopular.

8th September 1534

A letter from Mama says Catherine's health is much worse now. She barely eats anything, and the constant pain makes it hard for her to sleep. I had suspected this to be true, for I heard that Lady Willoughby, once Maria de Salinas, after whom my little daughter is named, had begged the King for permission to visit her old friend. He would not allow it.

I was glad to remain behind when the court went on progress this summer. It has been good to have some time with Tom and Michael and baby Maria in peace, free of the tensions and rumours of court life. I have been busy, of course, helping with the big task of cleaning and refurbishing the castle here at Windsor, ready for another year's occupancy, but I am not troubled by that. Fresh whitewash and the smell of new rushes bring their own cheerfulness.

2nd October 1534

The court is back, buzzing and twittering like the swallows that gathered a week or two ago before they flew off in the other direction, away from the English winter. Anne Boleyn's elder sister Mary is here, pregnant by her new and undistinguished husband, William Stafford. She married him secretly, and her father is furious, but she seems very happy.

Pope Clement died on 26th September. The new Pope has not yet been elected, but whoever he is, I am sure he will be shocked by what is going on here. Pig-face Cromwell has started a tour of inspection of all the convents and monasteries, and is closing many of them, confiscating their wealth for the Crown. The King approves of this. With the lavishness of his court life, I am sure he will find the money welcome.

8th October 1534

Anne's sister, Mary Boleyn, has been dismissed from the court. Her father so disapproved of her undistinguished second marriage that he cut off her allowance – and Anne then banished her. What kind of sisterly love is that? Mary did not seem concerned. I heard her say she would rather beg for bread with a good man at her side than be Queen of England. Rumour has it that she is going to put this in a letter to Pig-face! Anne is looking greatly annoyed, and I am sure someone has told her what her sister said.

17th October 1534

One of the grooms told Tom a dreadful story today. The King had been to see little Elizabeth, and when he was riding near Eltham Palace, he overtook a man called William Webb, who was riding a horse with his pretty sweetheart mounted behind him. Henry leaned across without a word to the man and dragged the girl over to his own saddle. Then he turned his horse and set off back to the Palace with her. This is not the first time he has done such a thing. These days he is indifferent to Anne's rages.

18th November 1534

Chabot de Brion, the Admiral of France, is here on a state visit. There is talk of a betrothal between little Elizabeth and one of the French king's sons, so there was a great banquet in the Admiral's honour. Anne sat beside her husband, richly dressed and trying her best to look sparkling and attractive. She has never been recognized as Henry's wife by the French, and she hopes through this engagement to be acknowledged as the rightful Queen of England. However, she looks much older now. Her pale face is beginning to set into bitter lines, and she seems scrawny rather than slim. Worst of all, she does not have the good sense to control her fury with Henry.

At one point during the ball that followed the feasting, the King went to fetch the Admiral's secretary from across the big room, and on his way paused to talk to a pretty woman. Anne saw this and burst into angry laughter. The Admiral thought she was laughing at him, and was about to take great offence, so she had to explain. "My husband went to fetch your secretary," she said, "but he met a lady who made him forget about it!" And she went into another peal of mirthless laughter. It was horribly embarrassing.

30th December 1534

This has been a difficult Christmas. It began with a shouting match between Anne and her own uncle, the Duke of Norfolk. This is not the first time they have quarrelled. I was not close enough to hear what Anne said, only that she was shouting at him in a temper – but I did hear the Duke call her dreadful names. He afterwards complained to Henry that Anne had used words to him "that should not be used to a dog", and the King was more than ready to believe him.

Anne speaks far more lovingly to her canine friends than she does to most human beings, including her husband, and there was a second Christmas calamity when her favourite dog died. She adored him and called him Little Purkoy, from the French word "*pourquoi*", meaning "why", because he had such an enquiring expression. Nobody dared tell her he was dead, and eventually the King had to break the news himself. There was much weeping and lamentation.

Now that baby Maria is a little older, Madam Anne commands my presence as an entertainer again. I have been playing and singing all day today with the other musicians, trying to bring some joy to this tense and gloomy house. I urged Mark Smeaton to look merry as he played, but he is far too nervous of the royal moods to risk anything as rash as a smile. Anne used to flirt with him before she became so bitter, but he never seemed sure how to respond, having little wit and no lightness of touch. I have heard him boast that the Queen is secretly in love with him, but nobody takes that seriously. All musicians know their listeners sometimes fall in love with the music and think themselves in love with the player. Papa used to laugh about it. "A professional hazard," he used to say. But Mark, poor thing, has little sense of humour.

8th February 1535

Anne has suggested Madge Shelton as the King's new mistress! She cannot stop his philandering, so she is trying to have a controlling hand in it. We are all vastly amused. Madge, to my amazement, is delighted by the idea. Myself, I would hate to get mixed up in the dangerous politics of being a royal mistress – and besides, Henry is not what he was. He is putting on weight, and complains often of headaches. The old sore on his leg has developed into an abscess, and has to be bandaged all the time. I have helped change the dressings myself sometimes, and the smell of the open wound is very bad. The King is in constant pain with it, which does not improve his temper. But I suppose Madge will put up with such disadvantages for the sake of royal favours and presents.

19th February 1535

Madge goes about with a smug smile, and the King looks pleased with himself. Anne, on the other hand, seems more wretched every day. Her mouth is pinched in suspicious bitterness, and her dark eyes have lost their lustre, narrowed between puffy lids. It was a mistake to choose a lady so well known to us as her husband's mistress – it has made her a laughing stock.

17th March 1535

Anne finds she is pregnant again, so she looks more cheerful. The King is paying more attention to her since she announced this news, and his interest in Madge Shelton seems to be waning.

7th May 1535

Three days ago, the Prior of Charterhouse Monastery was hanged, drawn and quartered, and so were four monks of the same Carthusian order. They paid the penalty for refusing to take the oath of allegiance to Henry's new Church. I feel cold and sickened at the thought of it.

In spite of the executions, John Fisher has again refused to take the King's oath, and so has Sir Thomas More. The two of them are still in the Tower. Anne Boleyn is urging the King to put them to death, but both these men are old and trusted friends. Mama told me once that Thomas More used to take Henry up to the roof of Greenwich Palace when he was a boy, to look at the stars. The pair of them shared a passion for astronomy, and More taught young Henry all he knew about the heavenly bodies. Surely the King must remember that? But it seems that Henry has no cares now for old memories or human decencies. He will condemn his old friend for the sake of his new religion. I pray for Thomas More, and admire his courage in holding to the true faith.

Anne is trying hard to improve her popularity with the people. She gives money to the poor, and when she visits a town or village, she sends her stewards ahead to find out if there are widows or destitute people in special need of help. She has provided for the education of several impoverished students at Cambridge – but when it comes to enforcing the new religion, she urges the King on in his cruelties.

22nd June 1535

John Fisher was beheaded at the Tower this morning. He was 76 years old. I wish Henry could have allowed him the dignity of a natural death in the fullness of time.

More Carthusian monks have been executed. This time the men were chained upright to stakes and left there to die slowly, in the humiliation of their own excrement. Londoners are not easily shocked – they watch executions as though they were fairground amusements, and walk past the rotting heads of traitors impaled on London Bridge with no more than an occasional complaint about the smell – but they found the deliberate brutality of these deaths appalling.

29th June 1535

Anne has for a second time lost her expected baby. It had seemed a healthy pregnancy, and at six months she was a good size with the child, so the cause is a mystery. Henry has little sympathy for her shock and grief. He is now blaming her for the executions that are making him so unpopular in the country, saying she forced him into them. Some whisper that he has begun to think Anne is a witch, and has put a spell on him to make him love her.

When love ends, does not everyone feel that a spell is broken? I cannot imagine ceasing to love Tom, but in moments when we have had some silly argument, I have felt bereft of love, and that is bad enough.

As to the question of witchcraft – how many women have been condemned by such a convenient accusation? It takes only the smallest abnormality or the slightest sign of being too clever, and tongues begin to wag about supernatural powers. It is very easy for Henry to call Anne a witch. She has a fingernail that sprouts beside the normal one on the little finger of her left hand, and they say there are warts on her body that could be the sign of the Devil. But the King did not object to these things in all the years he has declared Anne to be the love of his life, and he will need a better reason than that if he is to get rid of her.

6th July 1535

After a five-day-long trial, Sir Thomas More, the King's boyhood friend and lifetime adviser, was found guilty of high treason. He was beheaded on Tower Hill today. No words can express my horror and sadness.

11th July 1535

William Somers, the jester who took over when Papa died, went too far this evening. In a merry bit of fooling, he made some cheeky remarks about Anne and called the infant Elizabeth "a bastard". I was not present, so have no idea what he thought he was up to, but the results were instant. Henry has banned him from the court.

William is lucky. Until recently, such a dangerous joke could have cost him his life. Things have changed now, and the jester's instinct was right. Henry is no longer seriously angry with those who mock his wife. I suspect he is secretly pleased.

15th July 1535

The King of France has agreed that his third son may be betrothed to little Elizabeth, who is not yet two years old. Anne is delighted, and Henry seems pleased as well. The one thing the royal pair still have in common is their love for their red-haired baby, and they often go to see her at Hatfield or Eltham.

The summer progress starts soon, and this year I have to go with the court. Tom will be there as well, and we can take Michael and the baby with us, so I am quite looking forward to it. Little Maria is fifteen months old now, and is almost weaned, and there will be plenty of other people to look after her if I have to be with the Queen. We are to go first to Winchcombe, then to various places in Wales, and back through the county of Wiltshire.

29th October 1535

The King has fallen in love with yet another serving lady. This time it is Jane Seymour, who was in Catherine's service with me. She left when the Queen was sent away to The More. I remember her telling me at the time that she was fond of Catherine, but she thought it more sensible to stay in the King's court. Jane has always been very sensible. She is rather plain and has no sparkle at all, which is probably why Henry likes her. She is as different from Anne as any woman could be.

We stayed at Wulfhall during the summer travels, the house of Sir John Seymour, Jane's father. He does not sparkle, either. He is sheriff of Wiltshire, Dorset and Somerset, and owns a lot of land, but he is no aristocrat, merely a wealthy farmer. He was greatly excited to have the King of England under his roof, and could not do enough to make us all comfortable.

There is a great scandal about Sir John. For years he conducted an affair with the wife of his own son, and they say he fathered her two children. His son found out, of course, and there was fearful trouble. For a long time the family was split by deep hatreds, but we saw no sign of that during our time at Wulfhall.

Since our return the King has been paying Jane Seymour a lot of attention, and most people assume she will soon become his new mistress. I am not so sure. Jane lowers her eyes modestly at Henry's advances. She seems quite incapable of flirting, and just looks very sensible and very good. This may be due to the advice of her brothers, Thomas and Edward, who are both at court. They know perfectly well that Anne Boleyn became Queen by remaining virtuous, and clearly hope their sister can do the same thing. I groan at the thought. Do we have to go through another tedious and troublesome royal divorce? Life at this court is constantly packed with drama, and there are times when I long for simple peace.

30th October 1535

The harvest has been very bad this year, and people are blaming it on Anne. They are sure that God is angry with their king for putting away his rightful wife, and fear that they are being forced to share his punishment.

Anne keeps urging Henry to "get rid" of Catherine. It is as if she cannot believe herself to be the true queen while Catherine of Aragon lives and enjoys the support of the people. I am sure Henry would like to see his ex-wife dead, but for very different reasons. He cannot think of marrying Jane Seymour with two previous wives still living. Even with all his powers, the complications of such a move are too awful to think of. But it would suit him nicely if both Catherine *and* Anne were to die. Perhaps Anne has not thought of that. Meanwhile, she has no hope of persuading Henry to bring about the old Queen's death. The people would rise against him in rebellion, and the Emperor Charles would be his sworn enemy. Our king is too wise a statesman to risk these things.

6th November 1535

The King's problem may be solved by natural means before very long. Mama's last letter tells me Catherine is desperately ill, barely able to breathe for the terrible pains in her chest. Mama is sure it is partly brought on by worry. Catherine has not enough money to pay the few servants left to her, and she frets about it continually. Weak as she is, last week she struggled to sit up and write to her nephew, the Emperor, begging him to send her some money. I doubt whether he will take any notice, as he is busy fighting the Turks. It grieves me that this great lady should come to the end of her life in this pathetic way, no more noticed than a beggar in a gutter.

12th November 1535

Anne let it be known today that she is pregnant again. The King is pleased, but not ecstatic. After two failures, he probably doubts whether she will ever give him another living child. We can all see he has lost interest in her. His eyes turn constantly to Jane, the modest little dormouse who might – who knows? – be good at having babies.

16th December 1535

This is Queen Catherine's 50th birthday. I still call her Queen, if only in the privacy of my diary, for it is the only respect I can pay her. How extraordinary it is that a queen of England should achieve half a century of royal life, first as a Spanish princess then as Queen of England, without a flag waved or a trumpet blown.

A letter came from Rosanna today with the good news that she is expecting another baby. It will be born next summer, in early July, she thinks.

She said that the Queen managed to leave her bed for a few hours the other day, and sit on a chair. Evidently Anne has been told the same thing, for she flew into a panic of rage and alarm at the thought that her hated rival might recover. She ran to the King, demanding to know why he could not bring about the woman's death, and threatening that she herself would kill Catherine, and Mary as well, if he had no stomach for it. Henry's face was stony. He has no sympathy, either for his first wife or his present one.

27th December 1535

Somehow we got through another Christmas, though there was little joy in it. The Spanish ambassador, Chapuys, who is deeply grieved by Catherine's plight, sat unsmiling through the celebrations, and the whole court is uneasy. Jane's relatives fawn upon the King, while the Boleyn supporters become daily more strident, quarrelling among themselves and blaming Anne for letting them down. They are such unpleasant people.

29th December 1535

Chapuys has had a letter from Catherine's physicians, asking urgently that he should come to see her before it is too late. It is whispered that the doctors fear she is being poisoned, and do not want to be left to decide on their own whether this is happening.

Chapuys went to see the King, and came out grim-faced, though with permission to make the journey. Henry had expressed no regrets about Catherine. He merely remarked that once she was dead, the Emperor would have no more reason to act against him. Chapuys rode off to Kimbolton an hour later. Pray God he may be in time.

8th January 1536

Catherine of Aragon died yesterday at two in the afternoon. The messenger who brought the news gave me a letter from Mama that was smudged with her tears. On the previous day she and the other ladies had helped the Queen to sit up because she wanted to write to Henry. She could hardly hold the pen, but she wrote of her love for him, and of her innocence. She said she forgave him everything, and prayed that God would do likewise. She bade him be a good father to Mary. And as a last gesture of defiance, she signed herself "Catherine the Queen".

The messenger told us Maria de Salinas forced her way past the guards, who had orders not to let her in. I am so glad of that. At least Catherine had her old friend with her when she died.

An autopsy was carried out last night, before Catherine's body was sealed in a lead casket, and a black growth was found on her heart. Her doctors are sure it is a sign of poison, and those who cared for her said she seemed much worse after drinking some Welsh-brewed beer. We will never know the truth – but thousands of people in England will be convinced that Anne Boleyn is a murderess, and perhaps not for the first time.

10th January 1536

Last night a magnificent ball was held. I found it distasteful, with Catherine not yet buried, but the King had no such scruples. When told of his first wife's death, he seemed merely relieved. Anne of course was delighted. She said, "Now I am truly a queen!"

The royal couple wore yellow at the ball, because that is the colour of mourning in Spain. Henry has ordered a fine funeral to be laid on in Peterborough, where Catherine is to be buried on the 29th of this month. Anne seemed happy, naturally enough, and the King paraded little Elizabeth before the assembled company, as if to underline that she would be the future Queen of England. Princess Mary should inherit the crown, being the elder of the royal daughters, but she will be ignored.

This morning Anne's gaiety had evaporated. She sent for me to play, but when I went in with my lute she was sitting by the window, weeping. I asked if there was anything I could do for her, but she shook her head. I began to play a quiet pavane, and after a while she dried her eyes. When the tune ended she said, "You are a lucky girl, Ellie. You have so much. A good husband. Music at your fingertips. Children." Her lips quivered again, and she looked away out of the window with its diamond panes. They were coated with frost, for the newly lit fire had not yet started to warm the room.

I began to play again, a galliard this time, hoping the faster pace would cheer her, and eventually she put away her handkerchief, but her face remained anxious and unsmiling.

I know the cause of her distress. If the child she is carrying should fail to live Henry will discard her, just as he discarded his first wife. Anne thought she would be secure once Catherine was dead, but in fact it is the other way round. Now the old queen has gone, Henry has only one wife to deal with – and Anne has none of Catherine's influence with the people or with the powerful families of Europe. She is more vulnerable now than she has ever been. Staring out of those frosted windows, she stared at a terrible truth that she can no longer fend off. She, like Catherine, may end her life alone and ignored. Her dream of glittering triumph as the Queen of England is turning to ashes.

12th January 1536

Catherine's household is to be disbanded. Henry sent men to collect all her possessions, apparently to help pay for her funeral expenses. Mama was much grieved. She did not mind so much about the valuable things, like the little clock set in a jewelled golden book or the double portrait of Henry and Catherine, but the small things upset her. "Why did he have to take her nightgowns and her slippers?" her letter demanded, "and even the little clothes she had set by for each of her hoped-for babies?"

There are other things to worry about, more closely touching our family. The King is sending all Catherine's Spanish servants back to Spain. Mama is distressed about this. She is 50 years old, and says she cannot go back now to a country she left when she was sixteen. Everything that matters to her is in England. My brothers are working here at Henry's court, so they will stay. Tom and I are here, and Michael and Maria. "I will never see them again," her letter lamented. "I will miss all their growing up."

Rosanna will go with her husband. Diego was born here, it is true, but he has always wanted to go back to Granada, where his parents come from. They themselves returned there some years ago, when Catherine moved into The More with her reduced staff, and they write often to Diego. He is full of longing to see all the things they describe – the Moorish tiles, the fountains, the oranges hanging on trees in the sunshine. Rosanna is excited at the idea, too. Little John will love it, she said, and how wonderful for the new baby to be born in a place of sunshine and warmth!

Mama must come and live with us, of course. I know she will never consent to serve Anne Boleyn, but perhaps there is some work she can do in the court. If nothing else, she is a wonderfully fine embroideress. Chapuys says he will ask Jane Seymour to have a word with the King about it.

24th January 1536

While jousting today, Henry collided with another rider and both he and his horse crashed to the ground. The King was unconscious for two hours, and there was panic that he might die. When the Duke of Norfolk told Anne what had happened she remained remarkably calm, but I wondered as I looked at her whether she was simply too shocked to speak.

This evening Dr Butts said the King was out of danger, but he is still far from well. The old injury to his leg is badly infected and steadily worsening, and he is in great pain despite our constant bandaging. He should not have been jousting, of course. He is heavy and paunchy now, and he has lost much of his athletic prowess, though he will never admit it. His good looks are fading, too. The flesh on his face has thickened, making his eyes look smaller, and his mouth is tight and bad-tempered. The red-gold hair that was such a glory has receded, and he is almost completely bald. At 46, he still thinks himself young and attractive, but it is getting harder for the rest of us to see him that way.

28th January 1536

Mama arrived this evening with a small trunk containing her few possessions. Diego and Rosanna are here, too. John is three now, a bundle of black-haired energy. They will set out for Dover next week to take ship for Spain. I can hardly bear to think about it. Tom tried to cheer me up, saying we will go to see them one day when the children are older. Perhaps we will. After all, Papa moved about all over Europe, earning a living through his playing and fooling, and I am his daughter. A long journey should mean nothing to me. But for now, there are practical things to be done.

Mama looks thin and tired, and her clothes are in a terrible state, shabby and much-darned. I will lend her a gown of mine until I can get some fabric to make a new one. It may be that Anne will let me have some since she has more silk and velvet and brocade than she can possibly use.

30th January 1536

Yesterday was Queen Catherine's funeral. The King did not go to Peterborough for it, and neither, needless to say, did Anne. In the morning a solemn Mass was held in the chapel here at Greenwich, and I was glad to see that Henry was in black. Anne wore yellow, and grumbled that such a fuss was being made.

That was only the beginning of a disastrous day. Later in the afternoon Anne came into a room and found Jane Seymour sitting on Henry's knee, and flew into a terrible rage. She slammed off into her own quarters, and stayed there. I was not serving her. Madge had kindly said she would take my place so that I could look after Mama, who has a bad cold after the journey, and so I only learned this morning what had happened.

Anne had a miscarriage in the night. They say the child would have been a boy. It is the worst of tragedies for her. Madge said the

King walked into her bedchamber where she lay sobbing and uttered no word of sympathy. Instead, he berated her for the loss of "his boy". Anne, of course, shouted back at him, even in her distress. It was his own fault, she said, for flaunting his liking for "that wench, Jane Seymour". Henry stormed out, saying she should have no more children by him.

Anne is trying to put a bright face on it today. Now that Catherine is dead, she says, there will be no more malign influence at work, and her next child will live. We were careful not to look at each other, but the same thought was in all our minds. There will be no next child. Anne Boleyn has had her last chance.

26th February 1536

Diego and Rosanna left last week. I managed not to weep, knowing it would make the parting worse. Tom reminds me that I saw very little of them when they were in Queen Catherine's service. "Away is away," he said. "It makes no difference whether they are in Spain or Kimbolton." He is right, of course. It's just that Spain somehow *feels* further.

The King left Greenwich a few days ago to attend the Shrovetide celebrations in London. He did not take Anne. Last week he sent Sir Nicholas Carew with a love letter and presents for Jane Seymour, but there were none for his wife, who is very cast down by this. She takes it as a sign that her husband truly means to divorce her. I am afraid she is right.

Among Jane's gifts there was a purse of gold, together with a letter. We all watched to see whether she would accept Henry's money – but she did not. She kissed the unopened letter with great respect then handed it back to Sir Nicholas, together with the purse. She fell on her knees and humbly bade him tell the King she was a chaste and virtuous woman. If His Majesty wished to send her money, she said, she prayed him to do so as an engagement gift when she had "a husband to marry". Her modesty is impeccable, but her intention is plain. She will settle for nothing less than marriage.

Meanwhile, she remains in Anne's service, and the Queen stares at her with bitter enmity. She would like to dismiss her, but she dares not.

1st March 1536

Anne gave me some heavy silk to make a gown for Mama. Even better, she agreed without any argument to let her work as a needlewoman, making and embroidering clothes for little Elizabeth, who is fast growing out of her dresses. Mama wanted to refuse when I told her of the offer, saying she would not work for "that woman". I was a little sharp with her, and pointed out that Queen Catherine is dead now. There is no point in continuing a fight that is ended – and the old queen would not have wanted to see her old and faithful friend cast into penury. Mama gave in, but she says she will only work for the little princess, not for Anne herself.

5th March 1536

Henry is back here at Greenwich. As soon as he returned, he told Cromwell to move out of his rooms adjacent to the King's own quarters, and gave Jane the use of them instead. He installed Jane's brother and his wife in the same suite, to act as chaperones, but it is rumoured that a door from Jane's room connects via a gallery to his own.

Anne is hysterical with fury. She slapped Jane's face yesterday, not for the first time. She has the right to chastise her servants, but this was sheer jealousy. Jane seems unperturbed. This morning, she was provocatively opening and shutting a locket containing Henry's miniature, and Anne snatched it from her neck so roughly that she cut the side of her own hand on its gold chain. I had to bandage it for her. She was weeping as I did so, and she leaned her head towards me a little, as if she would have liked an arm round her shoulders in comfort. I almost responded, for I know she is in great distress, but she is not a child like Michael or Maria, she is the Queen of England. So I curtsied and moved away.

2nd April 1536

Anne has had me with her every day in the past weeks, bidding me sing and play and make her laugh, but it is increasingly hard to keep up my own spirits. This queen has been cruel and self-seeking, I admit, but she is being discarded because she bore three dead children, which seems very harsh. I remember the words Queen Catherine spoke to me – "Every woman carries grief." Anne Boleyn knows that now.

7th April 1536

Jane Seymour has left Greenwich in the company of her brother Edward and his wife. They are going home to Wulfhall, though nobody knows why. Jane has been saying she is weary of the lewd jokes at her expense that fly round the court, but we all think there is more to it than that. I remember how Henry sent Anne away to Hever when his case against

Catherine was being heard, and wonder if he has some plan afoot. He spends long hours closeted with Cromwell these days, and I am sure they are plotting something.

The King is to dissolve Parliament next week, on 14th April. This is much earlier than usual. Tom says it can only be to make sure the Queen does not appeal to its justice if Henry seeks to divorce her.

23rd April 1536

Cromwell has been away from court for the whole week. He came back this morning, and went straight to see King Henry. Various courtiers paused outside the closed door, ostensibly to brush a crumb from a sleeve or do up a lace, but their listening brought them no hint of what the murmuring voices were saying. Rumours and speculation are rife, of course, but nobody knows what the King and his closest adviser are up to.

24th April 1536

Cromwell has been questioning all of us who serve the Queen, asking if we know if any men have visited Anne in her private rooms. I said with truth that I did not, but he went on pressing me. One of Anne's maids had reported several names, he said. I doubted this so much that I asked him who they were, and his answer made me gasp. He listed Sir Henry Norris, Sir Francis Weston and Anne's own brother, Rochford. Then he added a fourth man, William Brereton, and lastly he mentioned Mark Smeaton.

It was so absurd that I hardly knew what to say. Henry Norris has been close to the King for years, and he is the kindest and most courteous of men. I remember how he offered Wolsey his own room on that dreadful occasion when the Cardinal was left standing in the courtyard with no provision made for him – and it was he who relieved Henry of his squawking peacock and pelican not so long ago. Sir Francis Weston has no eyes for anyone but his young wife and his baby son, and I told Cromwell this. He asked if I knew William Brereton, but I did not. Then he said I could hardly deny that I knew Mark Smeaton.

I told him Mark was innocent, but he was not satisfied. He observed that Mark has a romantic manner of speaking and behaving. This is true, of course, but I explained that many musicians get into this habit, because people sigh over the sweetness of the lute songs and expect the singer to be as romantic as the music. I did not tell Cromwell what everyone knows, that the Queen often flirted with Mark as she flirted with many of the court gentlemen. All of us who entertain kings and queens accept that we have to wear a face of bright gaiety when a royal person is in flirtatious mood, even if we are tired or hungry or longing to lie down and nurse a headache. Mark, as a court musician, has to entertain the Queen and amuse her, but it means no more than that. I told Cromwell this last bit, because it seemed safe as well as true, and his small eyes kept a cold watch on me as I spoke. Then he said, "So Master Smeaton would do anything his mistress commanded." It was a twisting of my words, and I frowned. "We all do what the King and Queen command," I said. His lips tightened into something that was not quite a smile, and he wrote a note on the paper he held. I wish I knew what it was.

28th April 1536

There are rumours that the Privy Council is considering the matter of a royal divorce. Someone asked the Bishop of London whether Henry meant to abandon his wife, but the Bishop refused to reply.

I wonder if Anne secretly fears something worse. Two days ago she asked her chaplain, Matthew Parker, to be responsible for little Elizabeth if the child should be left motherless. I saw Parker as he came out of the chapel, and he looked shocked. I didn't know at the time what Anne had said to him, but it leaked out, as all secrets do in this court. I understand now why the chaplain was appalled, for the same horror and disbelief laid cold fingers on me as well. King Henry may be planning not merely to divorce Anne but to bring about her execution. The idea has run round like wildfire, and everyone is whispering in corners.

The King, of course, shows no sign of thinking any such thing. He plans to go to Dover in a week's time, to inspect the new fortifications there, and as far as we know, he still intends to take Anne with him. Tom will be with the party as well, in case of any mishap with the horses on the way. I will not be needed, but I am in the usual turmoil of packing and preparation, with Anne constantly changing her mind about which dresses to take and which jewellery to wear. We are all wondering now if this journey will really happen, or whether it is an elaborate pretence. Henry has always been a good actor, and at the moment he is all innocence. But a cat that has stolen the cream can also look innocent.

29th April 1536

The King met with Cromwell and all his advisers this morning. There was the usual drone of voices through the closed doors – and then we heard Henry shouting in absolute outrage. "I knew it! I always suspected it!" When he came out, his face was livid with anger and he stormed off to his own quarters without speaking to anyone. Is this acting, too, or is it genuine? Nobody can guess.

Cromwell looks pleased with himself, and all the men who had been at the meeting have an air of new and important resolution. But they are saying nothing.

30th April 1536

Anne walked her dogs in Greenwich Park this morning as usual, and I was with her, together with several of her other ladies. When we returned, we found a crowd of people assembled outside the palace. I asked a man what was happening, and he said an important meeting was going on and they were all waiting to hear what was decided. He glanced at Anne as he spoke, then quickly looked away.

The Queen did not say anything. She went straight to the nursery and gathered up her small daughter, who is here at present, then carried her out to stand in the courtyard below the King's window. She told all of us to leave her, but I watched from a distance and saw her gestures of entreaty as she looked up at her husband. I could not hear what either of them said.

I came up here for a moment of solitude, and to write down this strange event. I have a terrible feeling of foreboding.

Midnight, the same day

Mark Smeaton was arrested later this morning. They accused him of having adulterous relations with the Queen, and took him to Cromwell's house in Stepney for questioning.

I keep asking myself whether Mark could possibly be guilty. He played for the Queen in her outer room occasionally, and I once saw him give a sly wink to a friend, saying Anne was wonderful in bed, but I just assumed he was joking. Anne Boleyn would never look at a mere lute player with a skinny body and lank hair. Or would she? If he caught her at a moment when she was feeling bereft and lonely, it could have been possible, I suppose. Poor Mark will never have the courage to deny it, because he always agrees with whatever his superiors say. So far this has kept him in favour, but it will do him no good now. He must defend himself, and vigorously.

Again and again I wonder if what I told Cromwell has counted against him. "We all do what the King and Queen command." It was no more than the truth, and I meant only to affirm Mark's innocence. Did Pig-face interpret it as a tacit confirmation of his guilt? I cannot bear the thought.

Nobody knows yet what it was that so angered the King at yesterday's meeting, but the planned visit to Dover has been abandoned. They were to depart in two days' time, so to cancel it at such short notice must mean something important is afoot. Everyone says it is to do with Mark's arrest. If he is found guilty, then Anne will be found guilty too – for it takes two to commit adultery. I cannot help wondering if the whole thing is a trap set by Henry and Cromwell to ensnare the Queen.

Madge says that even if Anne has been unfaithful, it does not count as treason against the King, but if she and her lover are suspected of plotting Henry's overthrow, it does. And the penalty for treason is death.

Henry was stalking about with an injured expression today, as if hurt and astonished that his wife has made him a cuckold. This time I am sure he is play-acting. If he and Pig-face have devised this plot against Anne, then he is obviously not astonished at all. Yes, I think he planned it himself, and behind the pretended innocence there is a cold determination to rid himself of his wife, no matter if it costs her life and Mark's. The King has become a monster.

Oh, what a risk I take in writing such words! I hide this diary carefully, and pray that nobody finds it – but to write the truth, even secretly, is a small relief to me in the nightmare that is closing round us. I am beginning to hate this court. I wish Tom and I could be far away with our children, living as ordinary people do, knowing no more of these cruel storms than they do of God's thunder that sometimes shakes the sky.

1st May 1536

On this May Day a great tournament went ahead as though everything was normal. Anne sat beside the King on the royal dais, watching the proceedings. She seemed unaware that Mark was no longer at court. I suppose nobody told her of his arrest.

Henry seemed particularly irritable, but we assumed it was because he could not take part in the jousting. After the accident in January his physicians have forbidden him to take any further risks, and he hates being a mere spectator. Normally he would have led one of the sides in their mock war, but today their leaders were Sir Henry Norris and

Anne's brother, Viscount Rochford. I could not help remembering that Pig-face had mentioned both men when questioning us about the Queen.

Halfway though the afternoon, the King got up abruptly and left the royal stand. Anne continued to sit there alone, but she looked puzzled and uneasy.

When the last event was over, the King rode into the arena. Ignoring everyone else, he brought his horse alongside that of Sir Henry Norris and escorted him out – but not, I thought, in friendship. Henry was grim-faced, and Norris seemed mildly surprised, though he greeted the King with his usual affable courtesy. The two of them went off together.

2nd May 1536

This has been a terrible day.

Sir Henry Norris was arrested this morning, and sent to the Tower. He is accused of having criminal intercourse with the Queen. Apparently King Henry questioned him closely on their ride from the tournament yesterday, and was not satisfied with Norris's protestations of innocence. Even more grotesquely, Rochford was arrested on the same charge, though in his case it is also incest, for the

Queen is his sister. They say Rochford's wife, who is a spiteful woman and on bad terms with her husband, gave evidence against him because she has always been jealous of his affection for Anne.

The Queen was watching a tennis match at the time of the arrests and suspected nothing. She was smiling, and I heard her say to Madge that she wished she had laid a bet on her favoured player, as he was winning so handsomely. Then a messenger came, and announced that Her Majesty was required to present herself at once to the gentlemen of the Privy Council. Anne sighed at having to miss the rest of the game, but she got up obediently and went to the council chamber.

I was one of the ladies who went with her, so I saw what happened. Anne's uncle, the Duke of Norfolk, was waiting for her at the door, and ushered her in. The assembled gentlemen then told the Queen she was accused of having committed adultery with Mark Smeaton, Sir Henry Norris and one other, whom they did not name. They added that the three men had confessed their guilt.

Anne did not weep or protest. She seemed stunned, as if she did not quite understand what had been said to her. We were told to escort her back to her chambers. An armed man came with us, and when we had gone in, he stationed himself outside the door, on guard.

Anne seemed indignant rather than afraid. She was desperately concerned for the accused men, knowing they face the death sentence if adultery should be proved against them. Strangely, she did not seem to realize her own danger. Perhaps she thought the accusation too ridiculous to take seriously. After all, everyone in the court indulges in a little flirtation from time to time – it means nothing. Or perhaps it was like her worst nightmare come true, and she could not believe she was not asleep and dreaming.

Some of Anne's ladies are secret supporters of Jane Seymour, and they glanced at each other with small, malicious smiles. Anne was careful not to look at them. The rest of us did our best to reassure her. I have had no cause ever to like Anne Boleyn, but my heart went out to her today, and I gave her what comfort I could. Anne seemed to believe that everything could be explained and smoothed over, and recovered something of her old spirit. We accompanied her to the dining chamber, escorted by the man stationed as a guard, and she set about her food with normal appetite.

She was still at the table when the door was flung open. The Duke of Norfolk came in, together with Cromwell and several other courtiers. Anne rose and asked their business, and her uncle unrolled a parchment he carried. He told her it was a warrant for her arrest. She was to go to the Tower, and remain there "to abide during His Highness's pleasure".

I thought it astonishing that Anne remained so calm. Her voice was quite steady as she answered. "If it be His Majesty's pleasure, I am ready to obey," she said. And they took her away. We were not even allowed to pack some clothes for her.

The net continues to close. Riders have been sent to arrest William Brereton, whom I have never met, and Sir Francis Weston. He lives at Sutton Place in Surrey, with his wife and baby son. He used to play tennis with the King. *Used to*. I am already writing of him as though his life was past. I feel sick to my soul at what is happening.

Jane Seymour's supporters are openly gloating now. How quickly everything has changed! Until a few months ago, every English citizen was being forced to swear allegiance to Anne Boleyn, and people were executed for refusing. Among ourselves, it was dangerous to express anything but the warmest liking for the Queen. And now she is suddenly the witch who enchanted the King then betrayed him, a wicked woman who plotted his downfall while sleeping with his enemies.

Tom and I walked down the grassy hill here at Greenwich to the river this evening, enjoying the fading daylight. Now that Mama is here we get away by ourselves more often, as she loves to be with the children. We met Will Cook, one of the Queen's bargemen, and he told us what happened this afternoon. Anne was escorted aboard at five o'clock, in full view of a great crowd of people standing round and gawping. Will was angry about that. Prisoners for the Tower are usually ferried there at night, he said, in the privacy of darkness, so why should she be denied this small mercy? Will has always shared the common view that this queen is a jumped-up harlot, but he was touched by Anne's plight today.

"That uncle of hers," he said. "For twopence I'd have tipped him in the river. Every minute of the way, he kept telling her the men accused have admitted their guilt. He seemed to glory in it. The lady never answered. Kept her mouth closed, stared anywhere but at him."

She collapsed when they reached the watergate at the Tower, though.

All the strength had gone out of her, Will said, and he and the other men had to help her up the steps to where the Constable of the Tower stood waiting with his men. She sank on her knees, praying for God's help and swearing she was not guilty. She was weeping, and she asked, "Mr Kingston, do I go into a dungeon?"

Sir William Kingston is the Constable. He assured Anne she would be housed in the quarters she and Henry had occupied on the night before her coronation. She said, "It is too good for me," and burst into hysterical laughter mingled with tears. It must have been terrible for her, remembering that glorious day a scant three years ago, when the river was all aflutter with crimson and gold, and music rang out across the water. It must have been a bitter contrast with the darkness that faces her now.

Will said she managed to calm herself a little, and then she said, "May God bear witness there is no truth in these charges. I am as clear from the company of man as from sin." I am sure she speaks the truth. She has been guilty of her own cruelties, but she is not stupid. She would never have done anything which so obviously would lead to her downfall.

It grieves me that the ladies serving Anne in the Tower are not her friends. One of them is the Constable's wife, Lady Kingston, and there are two of her aunts who have never liked her. The fourth is a Mrs Cosyn, who is the wife of Anne's Master of Horse. They have been picked, I suspect, to watch the Queen rather than to serve her, and to report on any admission of her guilt. There is also Margaret Wyatt, sister to the poet who once loved Anne. Perhaps her only true friend among them is old Mrs Orchard, who was her childhood nurse. I am glad she is there.

3rd May 1536

Henry Fitzroy, the King's son by Bessie Blount, was at supper with his father this evening. When he stood up to say goodnight, the King took the young man in his arms, with tears in his eyes. He thanked God that young Henry and his half-sister, Mary, had escaped death at the hands of "that cursed and venomous whore, who tried to poison you both". He spoke as if he really believed his own words.

Young Henry does not look well. He has a constant cough, and sometimes lays his arm across his chest as if there is a pain in there. I think he has consumption. They can hardly blame Anne Boleyn for that.

7th May 1536

Yesterday we moved from Greenwich to Hampton Court. This will be more convenient for the King to visit Jane, who is now installed at Beddington Park, in Surrey. His Majesty is growing his beard again. Anne preferred him clean-shaven, but it is Jane Seymour's wishes that count now. Ever since Anne was imprisoned, Henry has been in a mood of wild celebration. He runs from one party to another, celebrating and carousing. But no doubt he finds time for Jane.

12th May 1536

Today has been dreadful. I had to go to Westminster Hall as a witness in the trial of poor Mark Smeaton, together with Norris, Brereton and Weston. The case against Anne and her brother will be heard after the weekend, at the Tower. We left Hampton Court early to get to Westminster, and the accused men were brought from the Tower by river.

Mark looked gaunt and thin, drained of all hope. It is whispered that he was put on the rack at the Tower, and tortured until he confessed. I hope that is not true. Mark would probably confess of his own accord, and I thank God for it. He is not a hero by nature – and what would be the point in incurring further suffering? Protestations of innocence would be useless. The grand plan does not allow for them. Mark has to be guilty.

I said I knew of no misconduct by any of the accused men. I was careful about my words, lest they be misused, and was quickly dismissed as being of no interest. Some of the ladies gave the court far more pleasure, retailing salacious stories of the Queen's promiscuity. Nobody queried the tales they told, even though some of the alleged offences were remembered – or misremembered – from years ago.

We all knew the men would be found guilty, but the manner of their execution is the barbaric one reserved for those committing high treason. Mark and the other three will be hanged, cut down while still alive, castrated and disembowelled. Their bodies will then be cut into quarters. Dear God, grant them a speedy escape of the spirit from such agony. May they rest in peace.

13th May 1536

The King commanded today that Anne's household at Greenwich is to be broken up and dispersed. Those of us who served her are all dismissed.

I do not know what Tom and I will do. Will the King want me to serve Jane Seymour? It is plain that he means to marry her as soon as Anne is out of the way. After little more than a week, he is tired of riding out from Hampton Court to see Jane in the Surrey house. He is removing himself to Whitehall tomorrow, and Jane is to take up residence at a house in the Strand, just a short walk away.

This may be the right time to leave the court and all its intrigues. I suspect that I am pregnant again, and I am in no mood to attend to the whims of yet another royal mistress. Jane Seymour irritates me in a way that Anne, for all her malevolence, never did. Jane has large, rather stupid eyes and a little mouth set above a weak chin. She looks as humble and stupid as a sheep. I suppose that is what the King likes about her. She has a certain obstinacy about getting her own way, but she always appears utterly meek. She is poorly educated and has not the wit to argue with anyone, let alone Henry. He will have no trouble in getting total obedience from Jane. But I find her just plain boring.

Tom and I have dreamed for years of a small place where we can live peacefully with our children, but the dream seems difficult and almost frightening now that we must think about turning it into reality. My brothers have been told they can go on working at Henry's court. William is pleased, for he likes his work in the kitchen. He helps with the cooking now, and especially loves preparing the spiced cakes and sugared fruits that look so delectable at banquets. He is neat-fingered and quick, and he is happy in the heat and the smell of spices and roasting meat. Daniel is different. He is impatient with the court, too blunt by nature to make a success of working there. He wants to come with us, and I am glad of it. He will be useful, helping Tom in the forge and with the field-work.

Mama does not say much. I wonder if she is secretly a little dismayed by our plans to abandon court life. She has lived in the abundance – and sometimes the meanness – of royal households all her life, and leaving it perhaps frightens her a little. But there is nothing for her in Henry's court now. She has never forgiven the King for his treatment of Catherine, and although she has no sympathy for his new wife, Anne's fate confirms Mama's conviction that Henry has lost all humanity.

I am not sure she is right about this. It seems to me that the King is all too human when it comes to his own feelings. The trouble is, he fails to see that other people share the same worries and pains as he does. But at any rate, Mama says she would not stay even if Henry asked her. I am glad of this, for I would not like her to be regretting a lost way of life. She has had a hard time in these last years, and I think she will be happy with us once she gets used to the big change that has to happen. She loves the children, and they adore her. We must look for a place that has a good piece of land, then we can graze a cow and keep a pig and some chickens, and grow vegetables. Tom's trade as a blacksmith will bring in enough money for our other needs, especially with Daniel helping. But nothing can be done until the last scene of poor Anne's life has been played out.

15th May 1536

I went to the Great Hall of the Tower this morning for the Queen's trial. I did not want to be there, but Mama was determined to go. She still blames Anne for the ruining of Catherine's marriage, and said she wanted to see justice done. I was not sure if one could call the proceedings justice, but I could not refuse her. I certainly would not let her fight her way through those crowds on her own.

Men must have been working through the whole weekend to put up the central platform and the tiers of benches that surrounded it. At least 2,000 people were crammed into the place, all of them as agog with excitement as though they were at a circus. The Duke of Norfolk sat on a throne under a grand canopy, for he represented the Crown. King Henry was not present, and neither was Jane Seymour.

Chairs were provided for the 26 peers who were to judge Anne's case. The chief executioner stood at the entrance, holding his axe between his feet. Its blade was turned away, to show that Anne was not yet condemned.

I had been afraid they might have to assist her in, weeping and trembling, but Anne made her entrance with great dignity. She curtsied to the judges, and stared round at the assembled crowd as though she found it fascinating that so many people were present. Then she moved to the chair in the centre of the platform, and seated herself on it with complete composure.

The long list of charges was read out, and after each one Anne declared her innocence. She spoke clearly and firmly, and people were impressed. In the murmur that followed one of her statements, I heard a man behind me say, "She will see them off yet." I turned to look at him, but his companion was smiling grimly. "No chance," he said. "They have to condemn her. The King wishes it. And Cromwell stands to lose his own head if the Queen walks out of here a free woman."

All 26 of the noblemen declared her guilty. Anne still held her head high, as though she had faced the fact already, and conquered her fear. The Duke of Norfolk, on the other hand, cracked at the last moment. When he stood to pronounce the sentence his voice shook and tears were in his eyes. After all, Anne is his sister's child. The words he spoke have imprinted themselves on my mind:

Because thou hast offended our sovereign lord the King's Grace in committing treason against his person, the law of the realm is this: that thou shall be burnt here within the Tower of London on the Green, else to have thy head smitten off, as the King's pleasure shall be further known of the same.

There was an instant outbreak of talking and one or two people cheered, but louder than all the noise was a terrible scream from somewhere high in the tiered seats. There was a commotion up there, people trying to support a woman who had collapsed. I learned afterwards that it was Mrs Orchard, Anne's old nurse.

The Queen waited for the hubbub to be hushed, then she spoke. I will set down her words, too, as well as I remember them. She began by saying she had been condemned for reasons very different from the ones given. Nobody dared to nod agreement, though we all knew she was right. She went on to speak of the King:

I do not say I have always shown him that humility which his goodness to me merited. I confess I have had jealous fancies and suspicions of him, which I had not discretion enough, and wisdom, to conceal. But God knows, and is my witness, that I have not sinned against him in any other way.

She said that she was not trying to prolong her life. "God hath taught me how to die," she said, "and He will strengthen my faith." She spoke sadly of her brother and the other "unjustly condemned" men, and said she would willingly suffer many deaths to deliver them. Her last words were very brave:

> *Since I see it pleases the King, I shall willingly accompany them in death, with this assurance, that I shall lead an endless life with them in peace.*

She turned and left the hall then, walking between two ladies. The Chief Executioner now held his axe with the sharp edge of its blade turned towards her.

They found her brother guilty as well. The only evidence against him was that of his own wife. Everyone knows she hates him, so we thought he might be acquitted. He spoke fluently in his own defence, and things seemed to be going well for him, but then he was handed a piece of paper. He read the words written on it and frowned as if perplexed. A flush of embarrassment came over his face.

One of the lords said, "The paper is a statement allegedly made by yourself. Would you care to read it out?"

Rochford shook his head. "I cannot—" He halted, then began again. He was stumbling over his words, and I hardly caught what he was saying. "Create suspicion . . . prejudice the issue the King might have from a second marriage. . ."

The court burst into uproar. I turned to Mama and asked, "What does it mean?"

"That the King is impotent, and will have no more children with any woman," she said as the roars of outrage went on. "And if he wrote the words on that paper, he is a dead man, for they are high treason."

Rochford had just realized the same thing. "I did not say it!" he shouted, though his voice was drowned in the continuing rumpus. "I did not say it!"

I am sure he spoke the truth, and he had not written the words on the paper they handed him, but it was too late. The trick had worked, and Rochford was condemned. His death is to be the same terrible one that awaits Mark and the others.

The King is holding a river pageant as I write this, in celebration of his coming freedom from Anne. The palace servants started work a week ago to get everything ready, so he must have been very sure she would be found guilty.

I went down to the kitchen to talk to William, and he was with a giggling crowd of cooks surrounding one of them who was singing a scurrilous ballad about Jane Seymour. I had heard something similar being sung in the streets as Mama and I came back from the Tower. Londoners are enjoying themselves at the expense of Henry and his new woman.

I joined in the laughter, I must admit. Dreadful though it all is, the jester in me finds a rich comedy in the King's dealings with his royal wives. This evening though, I cannot help thinking of poor Anne, waiting to hear if she is to die by the fire or the axe. I hope, for her sake, Henry chooses the latter – it is more merciful.

16th May 1536

Anne has asked that her little niece, Katherine Carey, shall be sent to keep her company in these last days. The child is only seven years old. I would not like a daughter of mine to do such a thing. I can only hope little Katherine does not understand too much of what is to happen.

Cranmer was with the Queen this morning, they say because the King wants a divorce before she dies. I could not see why Anne should grant him such a request – it seemed no more than a last humiliation. But rumour has it that Cranmer told her she might be reprieved if she agreed to it, so she did so with great gladness.

I wonder if the King really means to pardon her? He seems to be of more generous mind now his plan has succeeded. He has amended the dreadful penalty on Mark, Rochford and the others, God be thanked. They will still die, but simply by the headsman's axe, with none of the grisly torture that had been planned. They will be executed tomorrow.

17th May 1536

Anne had to watch the five men die. She was taken to different quarters in the Tower this morning, with a window overlooking the Green and its straw-covered platform. Her brother made a long, brave speech to the watching crowd, they say, and all the men swore that both they and the Queen were innocent. Mark was the last to die. It must have been terrible for him, because the scaffold was awash with blood by then. He made no speech. He just asked the people to pray for him, and said he deserved death. We will never know the truth of what happened now. God rest his soul.

Anne's marriage to Henry was declared invalid today. I see now why the King wanted a divorce. Anne's little daughter, Elizabeth, becomes illegitimate once her mother's marriage to her father is broken. The same is true of Mary, the daughter of Catherine. With neither of the girls recognized as a rightful heir, the way is now clear for a child of Jane Seymour's to inherit the throne.

Henry has chosen to have his former wife beheaded rather than burned. He has sent to France for a skilled swordsman who guarantees to sever a neck with a single blow.

18th May 1536

The swordsman is not here yet because he was delayed on the road from Dover. A man who came here with a message for the King told us the Queen was distressed to hear of the delay. The execution was set for this morning, and she had hoped it would be over by now. The man said the Constable of the Tower assured her there would be no pain, and she laughed and put both hands round her slender throat, saying she had only a little neck.

I wish I did not have to hear such details. Like everyone else, I have seen many executions, and always thought nothing of them, but it is different when I know the condemned prisoner so well. I might have been in her place, had our paths followed different ways. I cannot stop thinking about her. I keep remembering the moment when she leaned her head towards me in need of comfort. I wish now that I had responded.

Ever since the death sentence, Henry has been behaving with a gaiety that most of us find distasteful. Perhaps he does not want to be alone with his conscience. Whatever the reason, he has plunged into constant parties and celebrations, with musicians playing and much feasting and drinking. I myself have been summoned several times to play for him. I reminded him yesterday that I am officially dismissed, but he just shrugged his heavy shoulders. Music, he said, speaks more sweetly than words.

19th May 1536

It is over. Anne Boleyn, Queen of England, died this morning at nine o'clock. The King did not witness her execution, and neither did the Duke of Norfolk. I was there with Mama. She insisted on seeing the end of "that woman" – for the sake of Queen Catherine, she said. Tom kept the children in the smithy with him. They always like the smoke and the clanging iron and the patient horses.

The time of the execution was supposed to be a secret, but a huge crowd of people had crammed onto the green in the centre of the Tower. The scaffold had been built high, so that everyone could see, and it was draped with black cloth and scattered with straw. The heavy wooden block stood in the centre, with a lot of straw at its base. The executioner wore black clothes, with a hood that covered his head and a mask over his face, as if he was taking part in some grim carnival. There was no sword in his hand, and a man beside me said it was hidden in the pile of straw behind him. He was right – when I looked carefully I could see the hilt sticking out. A priest stood ready, murmuring prayers.

The crowd hushed its chatter as the procession came out onto the green led by Sir William Kingston, the Constable of the Tower. Four ladies followed Anne – the same four who had been watching over her in these last days. The Queen wore a crimson kirtle and a gown of black damask with a low square neck, and her dark hair was bound high about her head, with a French hood over it. Every one of the people present must have been staring at her white neck, as I was myself. I will never forget how pure it looked, and how vulnerable. She kept glancing behind her, as if certain that someone must at any moment come to tell her this thing was not going to happen – that Henry had forgiven her and all was well. It saddened me, for I knew nobody would come.

Anne climbed the steps to the scaffold, followed by her ladies. Although none had been a friend to her, they looked distressed now, and Lady Lee, Thomas Wyatt's sister, was in tears. Anne spoke to them kindly, begging their pardon for any harshness of hers and wishing them happiness in serving their next mistress. Then she turned to the Constable and asked him to give her time to make her last statement. He inclined his head in permission, and she addressed the crowd. She spoke very clearly, again swearing she was innocent of any wrongdoing.

Kingston then gave her a purse containing money for the executioner. It seemed terrible to me that the Queen had to pay the man who was going to kill her. The black-clad man knelt before her, asking pardon for what he had to do, and she handed him the purse with complete composure, as though she were giving alms to the needy. He got to his feet and stepped back, bowing in thanks. Then he retreated to stand by the pile of straw.

Anne gave the prayer book she had been holding to Lady Lee, who wept afresh. The other three ladies helped her take off her necklace and her French hood. They tied a blindfold over Anne's eyes, then assisted her to kneel down. They had to guide her hands so she could locate the block and lower her head across its central ridge.

The whole assembled crowd knelt as well, out of respect, and when the shuffling stilled, we could hear the Queen praying aloud, "Jesus, receive my soul! O Lord God, have pity on my soul! To Christ I commend my soul!" She repeated the words again and again while the executioner quietly took his sword from the straw and came to the block. He raised the blade high, and it fell so fast that we hardly saw the movement.

The black-clad man retrieved the head from where it lay in the straw, and held it up to show the crowd. In his heavy French accent, he pronounced the formal words as best he could, "Zus perish all ze King's enemies." Nobody was listening to him. The lips of the dead Queen were still moving as though her prayer continued, and several people cried out in horror. The Tower guns fired as a signal that the execution had been carried out, and the crowd began to move away, very quietly. There had been no rejoicing for Anne when she was crowned Queen, but neither was there any triumph at her death.

I was in tears. I thought Mama would chide me for my softness over a woman who had done such harm, but she did not. "I have wished for her death many times during these years," she said, "but not on a trumped-up charge that she did not deserve. God have mercy on her soul." And we both made the sign of the cross.

I looked back as we left the green. Anne's four ladies were alone on the scaffold, weeping as they performed the last service for their dead mistress. I watched as they lifted her mutilated body and placed it in the arrow-chest that had stood behind the straw. Lady Lee was sobbing bitterly as she held a white cloth, ready to cover it. I turned away to join Mama, and we went out.

The remains of Anne Boleyn were buried this afternoon in the Tower's Royal Chapel of St Peter ad Vincula.

15th September 1536

This has been one of those golden autumn days, with the sky as blue as Michaelmas daisies. I spread the washed linen over the bushes to dry in the sun, then went with the children to pick brambles for a pie. We asked Mama if she would come, but she did not want to get her fingers pricked by thorns and stained with red juice. Besides, she said, she needed the bright daylight for her work, as her eyes are not what they were. We left her sitting at the cottage door, stitching at the little gown she is making. It is of fine white linen, pin-tucked and with embroidery at the neck and sleeves. It will be so good to have her help when the new baby is born.

The King was betrothed to Jane Seymour on the day following Anne's execution, announcing that he would marry her at the end of May – which he did. He was in high good humour and inclined to be generous, which was lucky for us. He listened with a benevolent smile to our request to leave the court, and made no objection. He even gave us a purse of gold, in recognition of the long service done to him and his family by Mama and Tom and myself, and this has been a godsend to us. We left the court a week after Anne's death.

I am glad now that I was not born a boy, as I wished so often when I was younger. For the time being, I no longer want excitement and change. I find tremendous pleasure in my children and in the task of making this tumbledown cottage into a warm home. The daily work is hard, but Tom and I share it between us, and Daniel's strength and enthusiasm is a big help. He is eighteen now, well able to take on the heavier tasks. Tom bought a horse last week, a good cob mare, six years old. The children call her Bessie. She is strong and good-natured, and as I write this I can hear Tom hammering at the plough he is making. Over the winter we can break a lot of new ground, ready to sow wheat and barley for the coming year, and more vegetables.

There are only a few pages left in this diary now, and I will keep them for special days in our family life. I pray that the King may be happy with Jane. I hope she will give him the son he wants, for only then will the fears and suspicions that fill this poor country be hushed.

May the soul of Anne Boleyn, who at the end was so brave and so undeserving of her fate, rest in peace.

Historical note

The date of Anne Boleyn's birth is not known, but it was probably around 1501–2. Some historians suggest a later date of around 1507, but this would only make her six years old when she entered court service, which seems unlikely. Anne's mother had royal connections, being the daughter of the Earl of Surrey, but her father was an undistinguished Norfolk tradesman. However, he gave his four children a good education, and Anne wrote in a beautiful hand, spoke good French and was skilled at music and embroidery. In 1513 she was sent to serve as a court lady to Margaret of Austria, Regent of the Netherlands.

The following year Mary Tudor, sister of Henry VIII, was betrothed to Louis XII, the King of France, and Anne Boleyn became one of her maids of honour. Anne's elder sister, also called Mary, was at this French court as well. When war was threatened between England and France in 1522, the royal betrothal fell through and the girls returned to London, where Mary Boleyn was briefly King Henry's mistress. When he tired of Mary, Henry's interest turned to the younger sister, but Anne already had a suitor, Henry Percy. The King ordered Wolsey to dismiss Percy from court. Anne was furious, and said so, for she never learned the wisdom of holding her tongue. She, too, was dismissed for her cheekiness, and spent a year with her parents at Hever Castle in Kent. She returned to court in 1524 or 1525, where she served the Queen, Catherine of Aragon, wife of Henry VIII since 1509.

Catherine, daughter of Queen Isabella of Spain, had previously married Henry's elder brother, Arthur, in 1501, but Arthur had died only six months later. This led to a long debate between various political factions as to whether her subsequent marriage to Henry was legal or not. Catherine adored her husband, but trouble arose between them because they had only one child, Mary, who would become Mary I of England. Henry desperately wanted a male heir, and his desire for a son made him impatient with Catherine. He had set his heart on a new, younger wife, and by 1526 he was wildly in love with Anne Boleyn. Anne was ambitious and clever, and she had seen from her sister's example that the King's favours could be short-lived, so she kept Henry at arm's length. This astonished him, and increased his determination to marry her.

In Catholic England divorce was unheard of, but Henry found a passage in the Bible stating that marriage between a man and his dead brother's wife was illegal in the sight of God. A long wrangle with the Church in Rome began on this point, and the whole case became known as "the King's great matter".

Anne's uncle, the Earl of Norfolk, saw that his family could gain immense power in the court if his niece should become queen, so he and his supporters were strongly in favour of Henry's divorce from Catherine.

Cardinal Wolsey, the King's closest adviser but also the Pope's representative of the Church, opposed this. Anne hated Wolsey, and in 1530 she persuaded Henry to have him arrested for treason. Wolsey died the same year, on his way to imprisonment in the Tower.

The Pope dithered and would give no judgement on the "great matter", being fearful of offending other powerful rulers, notably Catherine's nephew, the Emperor Charles, who dominated most of Europe. Henry was exasperated by the endless delays and began to lose all respect for the authority of Rome. In 1531 he separated from Catherine, sending her away to live in first one house then another, each a little smaller and less pleasant than the last.

In 1532 Henry granted Anne a peerage in her own right. Anne was not popular with the people, but she began openly to plan for her marriage to the King. Early in 1533 she became pregnant.

Although he had still not divorced his first wife, Henry married Anne in a secret ceremony within a few weeks of knowing she expected a child. The Pope threatened to excommunicate him, but by now Henry was planning with Archbishop Cranmer to establish a separate Church that would be answerable only to the reigning monarch of England, and not to Rome.

On Easter Sunday 1533 he paraded Anne through the streets of London as his chosen consort, but Catherine continued to insist that she, and only she, was England's crowned queen. The common people agreed with this, and resented Henry's infidelity to his faithful wife. Anne, conversely, was greeted with catcalls from the crowds wherever she went. A few weeks later, Cranmer took on himself the authority to judge the King's case, and declared Henry's marriage to Catherine null and void. With this final break from Rome, the Church of England was born – and Henry could consider himself a free man.

Anne Boleyn was crowned on 1 June 1533. On 7 September of that year, she gave birth, not to the longed-for son but to a girl, Elizabeth, who would become Queen Elizabeth I of England. None of her subsequent babies survived. Modern medical opinion suggests that Anne may have been rhesus negative, meaning that no child of hers after the first one could tolerate the type of blood circulating in its system. In our own time, such babies can be saved through blood transfusion, but for the Tudors, the condition was mysterious and fatal. Henry began to tire of his new wife, who was proving no more capable of providing a son than the discarded Catherine.

The three brief years of Anne Boleyn's marriage saw Henry's love for her turn to loathing. He began to look elsewhere, and in 1535 he fell in love with the meek and submissive Jane Seymour. However, with two wives still living, another divorce was out of the question. Abetted by his new adviser, Thomas Cromwell, Henry began to think of a more drastic solution.

On 7 January 1536 Catherine of Aragon died. Henry showed no great regret.

On the night following Catherine's funeral Anne Boleyn lost the baby she had been expecting. For Henry this was the last straw, and he raged that she should have no more children by him. Just over three months later a court was appointed to investigate charges that Anne had committed treason against the King by having illicit relationships with several other men, one of them her own brother. She was arrested and taken to the Tower of London.

At her trial Anne swore she was innocent of the charges. Her eloquence moved many people, but it could not save her. Both she and the men accused with her were sentenced to die. Anne Boleyn was beheaded on Tower Green at nine o'clock in the morning of Friday 19 May 1536. Henry VIII announced his betrothal to Jane Seymour the next day, and married her the following month, on 30 June.

In 1537 Jane gave birth to a boy, Edward, but she died of childbirth fever a few days later.

Henry subsequently married Anne of Cleves, then Catherine Howard, and lastly Catherine Parr, to whom he was still married when he died in 1547. None of these wives gave him any further children, and Henry was succeeded by his nine-year-old son, Edward VI. The six years of the boy's reign ended with his death in 1553. Catherine of Aragon's daughter, Mary, became queen, but she died after only five years, in 1558.

Anne Boleyn's daughter, Elizabeth, then came to the throne and ruled wisely and magnificently for 45 years. Perhaps in abiding fear of the fate that had overtaken her mother, she never married, and the Tudor dynasty came to an end with her death in 1603.

Timeline

1491 Henry VIII is born as Prince Henry, son of the first Tudor king, Henry VII.

1501 Prince Henry's older brother, Arthur, marries Catherine of Aragon. In the same year or the next, Anne Boleyn is born.

1502 Arthur dies.

1509 Henry VII dies.

Prince Henry is crowned King Henry VIII, and marries Catherine of Aragon.

1513 Anne Boleyn is sent to serve at the French court of Mary Tudor, who is betrothed to Louis XII of France.

1516 Catherine of Aragon has a daughter, Mary, later to be Queen Mary I.

1522 War is threatened between England and France, and Mary Tudor's betrothal ends.

Anne Boleyn returns to England and enters the court of Henry VIII.

1523 Henry Percy wants to marry Anne Boleyn, but the engagement is forbidden by Wolsey, at the insistence of Henry VIII. Anne is banished to her parents' home, Hever Castle.

1524 Anne Boleyn returns to court, in the service of Catherine of Aragon.

1525 Henry VIII begins to tire of Catherine, who has failed to give him a male heir and is unlikely to have any more children. He falls in love with Anne Boleyn, and plans to seek a divorce from Catherine.

1526 "The King's great matter" about his divorce begins. Divorce is illegal within Catholic England, but Anne Boleyn has powerful allies. The Pope fails to give judgement.

1530 Anne Boleyn persuades Henry VIII to arrest Cardinal Wolsey for treason. Wolsey dies on his way to imprisonment in the Tower of London.

1531 Henry VIII separates from Catherine of Aragon.

1532 Henry grants a peerage to Anne Boleyn. Archbishop Cranmer advises him that the "great matter" may be decided by the King and the English clerics, without reference to the authority of Rome.

1533 Anne Boleyn becomes pregnant, and Henry VIII marries her secretly, although he is still married to Catherine of Aragon. Following a judgement from Cranmer, Henry divorces Catherine, and the Protestant Church of England is established.

Anne Boleyn is crowned Queen of England, and on 7 September gives birth to a daughter, Elizabeth, later to be Queen Elizabeth I.

1534 Anne Boleyn's next baby is still-born. Relationships between her and Henry VIII begin to deteriorate.

1535 Henry VIII falls in love with Jane Seymour, and seeks to free himself from Anne Boleyn, who fails to give him a son.

1536 Catherine of Aragon dies.

Anne Boleyn suffers another miscarriage.

Henry appoints a court to judge Anne on charges of adultery with several other men, including her own brother. She pleads innocence, but is condemned to death.

On 19 May Anne Boleyn is beheaded at the Tower of London.

Henry VIII announces his betrothal to Jane Seymour, and marries her on 30 June.

1537 Jane Seymour dies after giving birth to a son, Edward, later to be Edward VI.

1540 Henry VIII marries Anne of Cleves, but divorces her the same year.

He marries Catherine Howard.

1541 Catherine Howard is beheaded.

1542 Henry marries Catherine Parr.

1547 Henry VIII dies.

Henry's son by Jane Seymour is crowned Edward VI, at the age of nine.

1553 Edward VI dies.

Catherine of Aragon's daughter is crowned Queen Mary I.

1558 Mary dies.

Anne Boleyn's daughter, Elizabeth I, comes to the throne and rules for 45 years. She never marries.

1603 Elizabeth I dies and the Tudor dynasty ends.

Picture acknowledgments

P 337 Henry VIII, Thyssen-Bornemisza Collection, Madrid, Spain/Bridgeman Art Library
P 338 Anne Boleyn, Mary Evans Picture Library
P 339 Hampton Court, Mary Evans Picture Library
P 340 Henry VIII at Hever Castle, Mary Evans Picture Library
P 341 Thomas Cromwell, Collection of the Earl of Pembroke, Wilton House, Wilts,UK/ Bridgeman Art Library
P 341 Cardinal Wolsey, Mary Evans Picture Library
P 342 Jousting, Private Collection/Bridgeman Art Library
P 343 Jane Seymour, Mary Evans Picture Library

A portrait of Henry VIII by Hans Holbein the Younger.

A portrait of Anne Boleyn by an unknown artist. Anne wears a necklace with a gold "B" and three pearl pendants.

A view of Hampton Court at the time it was first built.

A modern illustration of Henry VIII visiting Hever Castle, a family home of Anne Boleyn.

A chalk portrait of Thomas Cromwell by Hans Holbein the Younger.

An engraving of Cardinal Wolsey, Henry VIII's adviser.

An illustration showing a jousting tournament. Jousting is a sport where mounted knights attempt to knock each other off their horses using lances. Jousting was one of Henry VIII's favourite pastimes.

An engraved portrait of Jane Seymour, Henry VIII's third wife.

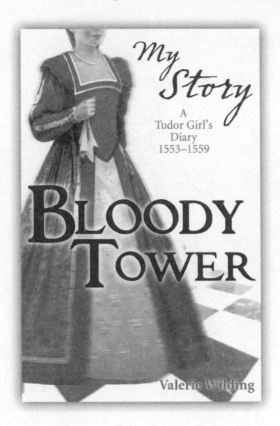

The sequel to *Bloody Tower*

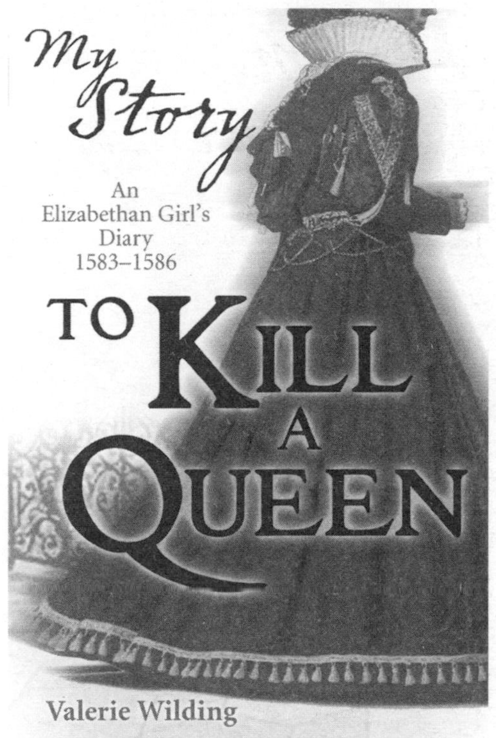

It's the 1580s. Queen Elizabeth's enemies plot to kill her and place Mary Queen of Scots on the throne. While Kitty's father works on secret projects for Elizabeth, her brother's mixing with suspicious characters. As Mary's supporters edge closer by the minute, Kitty fears the worst ... that they'll all be thrown into the Tower.

It's 1665 and Alice is looking forward to being back in London. But the plague is spreading quickly, and as each day passes more red crosses appear on doors. When her aunt is struck down with the plague, she is forced to make a decision that could change her life forever...

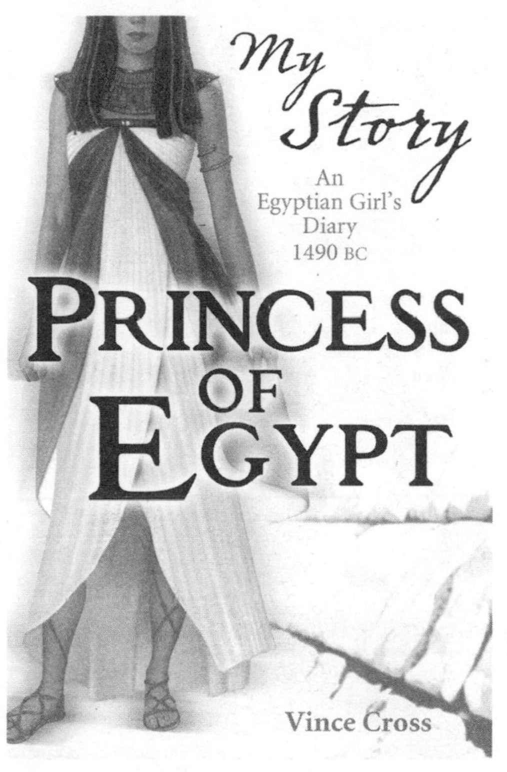

It's 1490 BC and Asha, daughter of King Thutmose, lives a carefree life at the royal court in Thebes. But when a prophecy foretells that 'a young woman will prove to be the best man in the Two Kingdoms', she's caught up in a world of plots and danger...

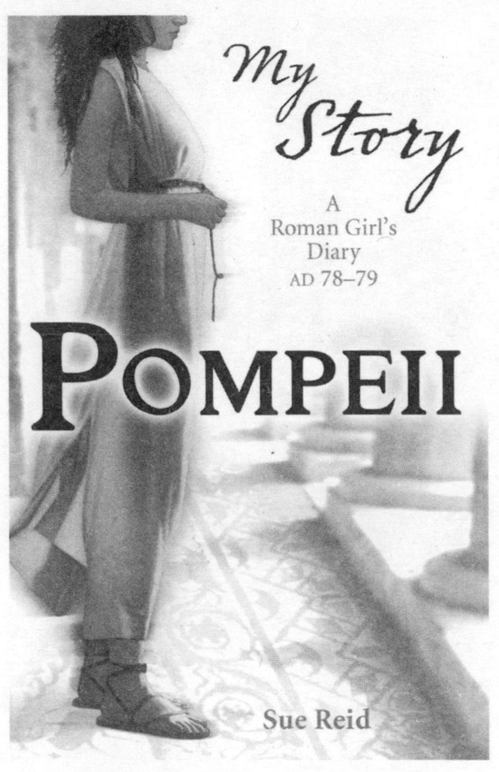

It's August AD 78 and Claudia is at the Forum in Pompeii. It's a day of strange encounters and even odder portents. When the ground shakes Claudia is convinced it is a bad omen. What does it all mean? And why is she so disturbed by Vesuvius, the great volcano that looms over the city...